Voices

and

Visions

ISBN-13: 978-1-958401-01-9

Cover art by Samson McCune
Interior design by Samson McCune

Give feedback on the book at:
samsonmccune@gmail.com

First Edition

Printed in the U.S.A

Contents:

Contents:

Part Of You

Layonna Gwynn

Losing a twin is like losing a part of you. From the moment we were created, our hearts beat as one. In two separate chests, maybe, but with heartbeats in sync. BA-DUMP BA-DUMP, the monitor sounded, "It's two!" our mother gleefully gasped. Embracing our father, happy too from the excitement of our existence. Two she had not been expecting, and Father was even more shocked. Nonetheless, as we grew from the size of a grape to the size of a grapefruit, the love we received was endless.

You had been on top in the womb, squishing me and taking so much room that I came out smaller. When we were able to finally kick and swing, Mom felt your kick first. I was more of a handprinter. I loved feeling Mom's warmth from inside our water sack. Whenever I would press my hand against the sack, her warmth would seep into my hand, making me feel fuzzy inside. As our ears began to work, Dad spent more time reading interesting stories. The ones that included the alphabet got you excited, KICK KICK; our sack would jiggle as mom laughed from your excitement. I liked the ones that included songs. I'd move really close to the front of the sack to hear our father's beautiful singing voice as he read to us.

Our gender reveal party was fun too. Both of us could feel the vibrations of the upbeat music blasting around our party. I was a dancer, you would get irritated and kick against the sack, but I didn't care how you felt. I would wiggle, turn, and flip at the vibrations of the rhythm. Mom had to sit down because of how active I was. She kept her hand on her belly so she could feel my awesome moves from the womb. Dad came over and helped Mom walk over to the gender reveal cake. Of course, I already knew what you were way before them. And you already knew what I was.

"It's A Boy and A Girl!" our father exclaimed, followed by the excitement of their friends and family.

"A two-for-one deal," our mother added and pressed a loving kiss on our father. Finally, after a long 34 weeks, it was time for us to come out to the world. You came out first, crying loudly, shocked from the sudden welcome into the world. Then I was pulled out, and I understood how you felt. Who, What, Why, my cries questioned. However, the moment we were bundled up and embraced by our mother and father, we calmed down and smiled as a greeting to our parents for the first time.

As we passed our first birthday, The smiles of our parents quickly turned into sighs of exhaustion in dealing with us. Moist pampers, growling stomachs, loud cries. Our routine drove them insane. You stuck faithfully to this routine day by day. I was more of the quiet baby, with wobbly lips and tearful eyes but hardly ever ear-piercing screams. That was until we started daycare for the first time. Separation was awful to adjust to. My loud cries shocked everyone in the vicinity, which made you cry, expanding it from the vicinity to blocks away. Mom had to take us home as we couldn't accept being left in an unfamiliar place all alone. The only thing that could cheer us up after that traumatic experience was the comfort of being rocked while lying on our mom's soft bosom.

By age 3, we were a mischievous duo. You loved the feeling of sticky food on your fingers and often, on purpose, spilled your breakfast on your clothes. Meanwhile, I loved dropping my breakfast on the floor and watching Mom pick it up while scrunching up her face at me. It was such a joy and often got a laugh out of both of us. Father was home less often; he got a new job, and his hours had gotten longer. He didn't kiss us goodbye before leaving in the morning, nor did he hug us when he returned. Mother and father also seemed to be becoming more distant the longer he worked. This hadn't bothered us until we realized he stopped wanting to read us our favorite stories to help us sleep at night. He had always used to read us and told us it was his way of increasing the bond between father and child. However, his new work schedule had made him less motivated to do so, resulting in angry and frustrated twins. Mother would try to pick up a book to read to us when Father refused. She would squish her lips and lower her vocal cords to mimic the wolf in the story or make her voice incredibly high, like helium, to voice the fairies. But this did not satisfy us twins and led to loud screams, tears, and a sleepless mother. You even got so angry one day our father came back and saw all of the pages ripped out of our favorite books. This was the first time we understood fear. He yelled at us and called us huge words we couldn't understand. This was also the first time we saw our mother angry at our father. So angry she struck him across the face. Our father did not come home that night.

By age 12, in elementary, we stuck together. Bullies had started trying to shake us for money. The only money we had was enough for our lunch. Living with a single mother, money had been tight, and if we had not eaten lunch, it meant no food for that day. Recess, lunch, homeroom, we were always together protecting ourselves and our money. That was until the day we weren't together. It was the day you were sick and had to stay home that day. The bullies drove me into a corner at school, and no one dared to step forward to help. Tears were burning my eyes, and pain stabbed my stomach from intense hunger. I refused to hand over the money that day. And because of that, my head was dunked into the toilet that day. Your eyes had mirrored our father's when we saw him angry for the first time. Despite being unsteady from your fever, you marched into school the next day. As though in a trance, you walked up to the bullies and punched the largest one hard in the jaw. The three other bullies grabbed you and started to kick and punch you in response, but you did not care. You kicked and punched back even if my voice had become hoarse from begging the fight to stop. Your fever sapped that last bit of your energy you had, and you collapsed onto the cold hallway floor. The principal ended up suspending you for three weeks.

By age 16, Mother fell sick. She was diagnosed with stage 3. You had to get a part-time job in order to help pay the rent and ease the burdens off Mother's shoulders. Hospital visits were tough too. Seeing our mom so pale, weak, and skinny, we prayed every day to God she would get better. It was mostly me that got the chance to visit her the most. Your part-time job was strict, and rent had been increasing too high for you to take time off. Even still, you worked the hardest; it was a shitty part-time job. The manager cared less for his employees, and the older employees pushed all their responsibilities onto the teen employees. You mopped the floors, worked extra hours, and never complained about your mistreatment. At most, you would bring home 120 dollars every two weeks. You knew this would not keep up with a roof over our heads, but you never complained. Not to me, and definitely not to Mother. But I could tell, beyond your smile, nothing was okay.

Two years later, on the day Mother would pass, three hours before her death, she called us both in. Holding each of our hands with her thin, pale fingers, she told us, "You two will always have each other."

Even if we spent months preparing for it. The pain felt worse than death itself. We were helpless to save her.

By age 19, I got pregnant. Ryan and I had been dating since I was 18, and we had one night, too many, without protection. You disliked Ryan, and he disliked you. Fighting constantly with each other, verbally and physically. It caused me grave anxiety about my pregnancy and about my relationship. Without you knowing, I went to an abortion clinic. The doctor had called me to the back to confirm my decision, but I couldn't move from my seat. For the first time, I felt alone and scared. Tears drenched my sleeves from my constant eye rubbing, and I felt a presence sit down next to me.

"Is this something you want to do?" You asked.

I jumped. Millions of questions about how you knew where I was and if I was truly committed to my decision formed in my mind. But my lips wouldn't move in order to vocalize any words.

"I'm sorry…" you said.

You moved your hand into mine and rubbed circles onto the back of my hand. I shook my head and held your hand back. We were scared. Him for me, and me for me. 9 months later, I gave birth to a beautiful son. When I gave you the option to name him, you named him Hope. "Hope is yours," You said as you watched me hold my first son.

By age 20, Ryan had left me to be a single mother. The responsibility had been too large, he complained. Even if every day I was the one up at 2 am breastfeeding, even if I was the one who rushed to the hospital when Hope caught a fever, even if I paid for the bills to care for him, zapping the last of my paycheck. However, I wasn't alone. You were there. The best uncle anyone could ask for. If I wasn't with Hope, you were. Watching baby cartoons with coffee in your left hand and Hope cuddled in your right arm. You took him to daycare, you would stay up with me at 2 am while I breastfed, and you would be there, sitting at the hospital with me, constantly reassuring me things were okay. Sometimes, I wondered if I deserved your kindness. But when everything shuts down for the night, and you leave to return back to your apartment, I look at Hope. Motherhood isn't easy, but with you and Hope with me, I could stay strong.

The day we turned 22, we had a huge party with friends. You stole the mic to the karaoke bar and enjoyed that you could sing Taylor Swift's 22 and relate. Despite you being tone-death and my ears bleeding, I danced to your voice. Our friends hyped you up in their drunken excitement. After your beautiful performance, you moved to sit next to your girlfriend, Amy. The both of you laughed and joked and cuddled on the plush seats. She made you happy. You two met while having the same lecture class in college and hit it off while joking about how trash the professor was. The chemistry had been strong, and I was happy for you.

On your first date, you were a sweaty mess. Asking me if

she would like this or that. If you should slick your hair down or rock the cute messy look. Rambling around, you were almost late for your date. But, thanking the time gods, you met her at exactly 1 pm outside the subway station. I almost didn't recognize you when you came over to my apartment after. Your face was red from all your drinking, your clothes all messy, and in your blubbery state, you said, "She is the one for me!"

On our 23rd birthday, a huge storm rained on our special day. Just like the storm, a storm grew between us. You promised you would pick Hope and me up from his daycare, and we could enjoy a nice dinner together. I was already exhausted from teaching dance at Rhythm Academy, but I was excited to finally spend time with you out of our busy schedules. Except you forgot, leaving me and your 3-year-old nephew stuck in the rain. I yelled and cursed you out for your idiocy. Saying words I had never in my life said to you. You told me to calm down, and you were on your way to get us out of the rain. I told you not to bother and hung up angrily on you. You sped up the car despite the heavy rain impairing your vision, and while making a right turn, you didn't see the large truck driving straight into you. The impact killed you instantly. While the car continued to flip and land on its top.

I didn't want to believe it. Amy called me and told me words I refused to come to terms with. I ran to the hospital, my heart pumping loudly over the heavy the rain. When I arrived, I was completely drenched from head to toe. Amy walked over to me, shocked at my condition, but I could not hear her words of concern. With heavy feet, I dragged myself to your hospital room. So badly I wanted to hear this was a joke and you were pranking me for our birthday. You would smile your goofy grin and laugh as you pulled the best prank of your life. But your body lay pale. Your eyelids did not flutter open. I lifted my dripping hands to your face hoping, no praying, you would react. But you did not. You were cold, colder than me, who had been in the ice-cold rain. The moment I realized you were gone, part of my heart stopped beating.

By 24, I said I was fine.

By 25, I said I moved on.

By 26, I said, please stop asking me if I'm fine!

When our 27th birthday came along, I made my decision to stop my heartbeat as well. Ever since you passed, I was in an endless circle of depression. Meds stopped working long ago, and therapy was more of a chore than an outlet. Once half the heart has stopped, was there still a reason for me to keep my half going, I thought many times on my own. I didn't cry at your funeral or at your grave the next year, or the next, or the next. I didn't want to cry. This year was going to be different. Before I headed to your grave for the 5th time, I packed extra pills for the trip. This time I was going alone.

You were buried an hour away from where the two of us lived this year. It wasn't because I was unwell but because I had to transfer to another Dance Academy for work. Amy hugged me tightly the day we moved. She wished Hope and me well with a smile and tear-filled eyes. Amy cried the most at your funeral. The two of us almost fought that day because she was disgusted by the deadpan look on my face as we watched the lid on your casket close. "We were going to have a baby, to become a family, do you even care!" she yelled, but I had no words of comfort to share. "He is gone," she wept.

A week later, she ended up apologizing and understanding that I was grieving the most. She even offered to babysit Hope whenever I needed a parenting break. She said she was here for me. But, I told her like I told everyone else who came up to me with tear-filled eyes, "I'm fine." With a smile that never reached my eyes.

I stopped, first at Amy's, to drop off Hope. I told her I was going on a business trip for a couple of months. Hope looked at me, but I couldn't bring myself to return his gaze. I felt nothing. My heart was set on leaving this world.

"Mom!" Hope called out as I reached for the door handle.

I didn't turn around. I couldn't. I wanted to turn my ears off and not listen. "Have a safe trip. I love you," he continued.

'I love you,' his words rang in my ear like fire.

The drive to your grave felt like days. Time passed slowly. My mind was blank, and the only noise I could hear was the engine of the car. At last, I arrived. My body felt heavy as I walked over to your grave. Fresh flowers and a can of beer occupied your grave. I looked at it with dreaded eyes and narrowed eyelids. Wishing time could be reversed. Wishing, why could it not have been me? Staring at the words imprinted on your grave, I took a shaky breath and pulled out the pill bottle. Popping open the lid, I poured over 20 pills into my hand. I had no regret. I wasn't regretting.

I wasn't until…I remembered the night before you died.

"Shh, you don't want your mom to wake up, heh."

You and Hope stifled laughs as you two decorated the birthday cake. It was a cake full of playful colors. Red, blue, and pink creatively splattered on the top. Hope had written a messy but legible "Happy Birthday" smack in the middle.

"You think she will like it?" Hope asked

"Of course! Who doesn't like cake? And even better, it's made by her wonderful son" You grinned and patted Hope on the back, getting icing on the back of his tee. In fact, the two of you had been covered almost head to toe in colors and flour. I wanted to come out and tease you both, but you noticed me spying from behind the wall. Without panicking from your ruined surprise, you lifted a finger to your lips. 'Shh,' you insinuated with your motion. I huffed and smiled lightly, deciding against my previous idea.

"I want to add more sprinkles," Hope said

"Aw yeah, add as much as you want."

As soon as Hope fell to sleep, I walked into the kitchen. You had already cleaned and gone back to your apartment for the night. I opened up the fridge and pulled out the cake. Scanning the beautiful mess you two created. Underneath the 'Happy Birthday' read, 'Hope luvs U'

My arm shook. The memory replayed in my head over and over. My knees gave way, and I landed on the moist grass in front of your grave. The pills spilled from my hand as I released my grip. A wave of grief and sadness passed over me, and tears stained my face. For 4 years, I had not thought about Hope, burying the love I had inside for him while avoiding his gaze as the days passed. I couldn't face him. I couldn't when my heart ached so much to see you again. I was finished with suffering from grief and made my way to your grave to take my life, but I couldn't do it. That's why I didn't understand why my heart ached now with the desire to see my son again. For the first time since you and I had sat together at that clinic, I wept. I drove back, my heart pounding so loud with anticipation. My arrival had startled Amy. She questioned how come I was back so early. But I couldn't answer. I instead walked over to my son, who was also shocked by my arrival, and for the first time in 4 years, looked into his eyes.

"Hope…" my voice shook with sadness, "I understand now."

I pulled Hope into my arms and wept. Hugging him tightly, afraid to let go.

"Hope, you are a part of me."

The Sea and the Sky

Alexander Templeton

The sun had not yet risen on the sleeping streets of the floating city of Sylva. The docks only had a single airship tied up, passengers shuffling out with heads hung in dreariness. The handful of workers finishing the night shift didn't bother pretending to look busy. Through the heavy lethargy of pre-morning, Sepers vaulted the low fence to the dock and sprinted towards the edge.

"Sep!" shouted one of the dock workers. "You do this again, I'm going to your ma!" But Sep was already at the edge and, without breaking his stride, threw himself into the open air. Far below, he knew the ground was staring right on back, but for now, it was swallowed by dark sky. For a second, he was in free fall, flailing his arms to twist onto his back. The net sank a meter as it caught him.

Officially, the net existed for the safety of the dockworkers and clueless tourists that might trip over the edge, but Sep had seen it catch entire cargo boxes, and it was the fastest way down into the guts of Sylva. He scrambled up onto a shallow ledge, then into a tunnel carved into the rock.

The path was lit with balls of green light jutting out of the walls, all fluctuating out of sync, though not quite flickering. It took him downward, deeper, and further into the cone-shaped island that Sylva proper sat on.

Just deep enough in that the outside world was no longer visible, the tunnel opened into a cavern wide and tall enough to fit several houses and that continued inward as far as the eye could see. Stores with big glowing signs lined either side of the cavern, windows of rooms unknown sat atop the storefronts and glared unblinkingly at him, and, every so often, shadowed tunnels snaked their way back into the rock. Down the center of the cavern, two lines of rail stretched out. At the base of them, an odd clockwork machine sat idle. Sep slotted in a coin, and it began to whir and click as various visible parts spun frantically until, at last, it spat out onto the right line what was, really, no more than a tiny chair on wheels. As he took a seat, another spinning gear embedded in the rail grabbed a hook on the bottom of his ride and shot him forward.

Rushing wind overtook the sound of squeaking bats that lined the top of the cavern, and the world turned a little less green as street vendors worked with open flames out of their metal food carts. Sep supposed there was ventilation somewhere by the bats, though no hole was big enough to ever let in any sunlight.

It was busier down here than the streets above. The usual suspects were on their way back home on the surface: An old man stumbling out of a tavern, dressed in princely attire now tattered and with a large beer stain on the vest; A group of women piling out of an establishment signed "GIRLS," their workday finally over; One of the few city guards that patrolled the under city inspecting a piece of graffiti to avoid dealing with a fistfight that had broken out, pockets already lined with enough bribes for the night. But beyond those, a parallel group of people existed to whom this place was home. To whom the day and night of the world above no longer meant anything, and there was no reason not to be awake at this hour. To whom the street vendors sold to and filled the damp air with sweet and spicy smells of every flavor.

It was easy to make out this new group by the disfigurements. One had glowing white eyes. Another had hair floating around their head as if it were underwater. A vendor shot sparks to light her barbeque with the snap of her fingers.

The rail took Sep past the markets to a more high-class district, in so far as the under-city could be high class. He leapt off as he passed a sign that read "Purdage University" that marked the servant's entrance and ran inside.

"Hi, Sep!" called out a handful of the cooks as he dodged through the crowded kitchen, snatching a pastry on his way out and up to the research section. Through a maze of windowless corridors, at last, he burst through the door labeled 'Dr. Hearend.'

"Sorry I'm late," Sep said through panting breaths.

"Never mind that I'm just about to finish fueling them. You haven't missed the good part," Hearend said. The laboratory was a fairly big room, yet every inch was cluttered with tables filled with strange metal devices in various stages of prototype. Sep had to dance around the layer of miscellaneous tools that had fallen to the ground. At the far end of the room, where Hearend was hunched over, were the two automatons he'd been assisting the doctor build for the past two years. Both roughly humanoid and with bodies of shiny steel.

The back panel of the one Hearend was working on was removed, revealing the infinitely complex system of tiny gears and pulleys that built the interiors. From a pipette, he was releasing drops of a glowing green liquid into one of the pipes in the automaton.

"Is that…" Sep started.

"The most refined ilum between here and the capital."

"Isn't it dangerous?"

"Any impurities in the refining process that might still be emitting fumes will soon be trapped in here," Heartened said, tapping the machine on the shoulder. He replaced the back panel then took a step back.

"Now what?" Sep asked.

Hearend raised an open palm to silence him.

The automatons jolted up to their full height. They turned to face Sep and Hearend. "Hello," the one on the right said, voice missing a few too many sounds to pass as normal. It had the same effect as listening to a song when the singing has stopped but still hearing imitation words in each chord of the piano.

"And you?" Hearend asked the other one.

It glanced at its twin, then back to the doctor and his apprentice. "Hello?" Hearend took a step forward, left hand raised as if to cup their metal cheeks, but not quite touching. He let the hand drop. "Well, good," he said and shuffled off to fiddle with some smaller project.

"They're beautiful," Sep whispered. "Doctor Hearend, you've done a miracle here. You've created... life."

"No, not quite. But the closest you can get to it." Only the grey hairs on the back of his head faced Sep, a gentle pinging of metal on metal emanating from whatever Hearend had begun to work on. "And now I need you to take them away. The mayor has requested the presence of both of them at a ball he is throwing next week. Would you kindly escort them to the palace to demonstrate they are now ready?"

Sep gaped at his mentor. "What, just like that? What's the rush, and why wouldn't you take them yourself?"

"Because that is the price of progress in this city!" Hearend turned on Sep with a start. "Do you know how expensive it is to craft to absolute perfection a million different gears? To refine even an ounce of ilum? The material, in its very essence, refuses to leave its gaseous state in any temperature or pressure. And yet I have tamed it! But those that fund these ventures care not for progress or impossible feats of science. This creation of mine could revolutionize the world. We could construct thousands upon thousands of these to do the jobs we cannot do ourselves. Whole new realms of possibility would be opened with workers like that! But no. Instead, it's... it's to be used as nothing more than a cheap party trick!" He was yelling now. "So no, you will take my place to go entertain the mayor, and I will stay here and work on my next invention because that is what I do! I am an engineer, not a circus master!"

Sep had nothing to say in response. After a minute of silence, he led the two automatons out of the lab and up the long staircase to the main floors of the university, where things were less prone to exploding and did not need to be hidden underground. They passed through the gargantuan entry hall and exited out the front doors into brilliant morning light. "Are you alright?" One of the pair asked.

"Fine," Sep said, blinking away the dampness that had formed as his eyes finally adjusted. He laughed and spun around to the automatons, raising his hands exactly as he imagined a circus master would. "Ladies and Gentlemen, welcome to Sylva!"

Cobbled streets were already packed with the business of the day, flanked by buildings of brick and wood, all painted in a variety of homey colors. And the sky, big and bright blue with only a scattering of thin clouds that lived this high up. The air was crisp and clean from the residue of winter colds. Fiddle and lutes and all sorts of foreign instruments rang out in overlapping melodies. Up the hill, towards the center of the city, proudly stood the great marble walls of the mayor's palace, crystal windows sparkling in reflected sunlight.

The automatons stomped down the streets in their unnatural weight, drawing the eyes of every passerby. Sylva was well accustomed to strange sights, but the bright polished steel of two independently walking machines still stole a lot of stares.

A bundle of guards let them into the palace, and after a short wait, they were ushered into an empty ballroom. The mayoress was waiting by a corner table, a multi-colored cocktail in hand. Sep hung back to let the automatons meet her on their own.

"A pleasure to meet you," she said, raising out a limp hand. Each of the pair grabbed the hand and kissed it in turn. Sep imagined it must have felt incredibly cold, but the mayoress showed nothing but amusement. She glanced back at Sep and frowned. "And where is Doctor Hearend, might I ask?"

"Unfortunately, he is attending urgent business," Sep replied. "But he asked me to convey his best wishes. If you have any questions regarding their make, I apprenticed with the doctor over the entire duration of their construction, and much of the time, they were being designed as well."

Very well," she said, turning back to the pair. "Do either of you have names yet?" "No, Ma'am," the one on Sep's right said.

"Well, we must remedy that! What would you like to be

called?"

"I don't know, Ma'am."

"In that case, your name shall be… Valo." She turned to the one on the left. "And you shall be…"

"Ariel, if you please, Ma'am."

The mayoress beamed at Sep. "I didn't realize they were capable of inventing new names like that."

"I heard it in a song on the way here," Ariel said. "I thought I ought to have a name of my own if that's alright?"

"I think it's an excellent name. There is another matter I'm curious about. As it will be a ball you two are invited to, are you able to dance?"

The two were silent until Valo said again, "We don't know, Ma'am."

The mayoress looked to Sep. "They're made to imitate people as closely as possible; I don't see why not."

"In that case, off you go!" She said, shooing them onto the dance floor.

The dance was clunky. Though it got a bit better as they continued, Sep suspected not even the greatest dancer could make much of a performance without any atmosphere or music or the color and movement of elegant suits and flowing gowns.

"Bravo!" the mayoress cheered as the dance ended. "These two will be wonderful for the ball. You must let the good doctor know his work is most profusely respected among high society. And farewell to both of you, Valo and Ariel. You are both most fascinating creations. Truly."

The automatons kissed her hand once more, then a guard led them back to the busy street. "Are we returning to the laboratory?" Ariel asked.

"Yup, Doctor Hearend will want a full report on what happened," Sep said.

"I have enjoyed this trip very much; I would like to see more of Sylva before returning."

"Well… I'm not exactly sure how long your fuel is good for."

"I would like to go anyway."

"Did you not hear?" Valo said, "The Doctor wishes us to return."

The two stared at each other. Ariel broke first and set off down a side street. Valo turned away and continued walking down the main road towards the University, leaving Sep standing in place, watching the automatons recede in different directions.

He hesitated, eyes flicking between the two of them. "Just uh… give Hearend a report for me, will you?" Sep shouted after Valo before taking off into the side street. He soon caught up with Ariel but had to half-jog just to keep up with their long strides.

"So, where did you want to go?" Sep asked.

"Everywhere."

"Look, I think you're a fascinating piece of engineering, so I'm happy to see where this goes, but I imagine Hearend will be slightly less excited at his life's work running away, and up here, you're not exactly difficult to find."

"What do you suggest?"

"Well, if you really want to see 'everything,' we gotta go somewhere you won't be caught so quickly."

"And?"

"And there ain't no better place to disappear than the under-city."

There weren't as many entrances to the tunnels in this part of town, but he estimated Valo had not quite gotten back by the time they found their way down. He showed Ariel the markets, tried to describe what it was like to smell as they passed a bakery, then brought them to a freak show with a lineup of people with strange magical deformities. A small girl flailed about in the air with insect-like wings for a minute before collapsing back to the ground. A gigantic man roared with the power of a jungle beast and shattered a row of windowpanes that had been set up.

After the show, the manager approached him. "You got a mighty interesting friend there, kid. I've known some guys that've been living down here a real long time, and none of them are close to looking like this."

"It's not a mutation. It's an automaton," Sep explained.

"Well, whatever it is, I'd be willing to pay a whole lot if it's looking to work." Sep looked up to Ariel. "It's your choice."

"I am afraid we do not have the time," Ariel said.

"If you ever change your mind, it's not hard to find us," the manager said and wandered back to his troupe.

"Why do people dance?" Ariel asked as they walked back through the green-tinted streets of the under-city. "Back in the palace, I understood how to do the moves but could not figure out why anyone would do them."

Sep giggled. "Well, 'cause you didn't have music, of course. In all honesty, it did look a bit silly. Come on. I'll show you!" Without waiting, he ran off in the direction of the faint sound of saxophone.

They found a crowd gathered around a small band of buskers, many of them already stomping their feet to the beat. A couple of people noticed Ariel but quickly turned back to the music.

"Go ahead, try it," Sep said.

Ariel began stomping their heavy metal foot as loud as the drummer himself, imitating the crowd. Now, the curious looks lingered on the automaton. Big smiles met Ariel's perfectly impassive face, and the crowd parted to give Ariel a path into the semi-circle around the band, slapping them on the back as Sep pushed them in. A smaller group had already started dancing inside, and a woman took Ariel's hand and led them into the chaotic dance that had the whole group changing partners every ten seconds.

A girl offered her hand to Sep as the song changed. He shook his head. "I'm just here to watch the automaton," he said, nodding toward Ariel.

"You can watch and dance at the same time," she said, keeping her hand out. "You make a good point," he said with a smile and took her hand.

Halfway through the dance, they came to a move where his partner did a small jump, and at the same time, he had to throw her up by the arms as high as he could. In the next measure, they swapped roles, and Sep glanced over to see what poor guy would have to try and lift Ariel. Yet as the measure ended and they jumped, Ariel was lifted with grace a meter off the ground. To his surprise, he realized that he, too, was still in the air with gravity that seemed not to want to bring him back down. All around, lines of green dust hovered and vibrated with the beat of the drums.

He looked back down to his partner. Her eyes glowed bright green, and her left hand was raised out behind her, tendrils of the dust slinking out from every finger.

"Your friend isn't the only strange thing to live down here," she whispered with a voice that echoed directly into his ears. The music returned to the chorus, and she dropped her hand, spinning him around her as gravity returned to normal.

Sep and Ariel found each other after one more song and began walking towards a cart that had some miscellaneous meat frying on it. "So, did you like it?" Sep asked. "No."

"That's too bad. What didn't you like?"

"I neither liked nor disliked it. But I wish I could have. I understood from the joy in that crowd why you people do it, and as I am constructed to imitate people as well as possible, I now know the flaw that I must fix."

"Yeah?"

Ariel considered him for a moment. "I need you to help me become alive." Sep coughed out a spurt of laughter.

"I am entirely serious in this wish," they said.

"And I believe you," Sep said. "It's just that I barely did a fraction of the work to get you this far. I'm not exactly sure how, or even if, it's possible to do what you're asking." "Nor did I expect you to. I do understand, at least in part, why you have come with me despite the risk to your career. You seek answers."

"So you're saying you've an idea of what to do?"

"I am." Ariel approached a lamppost containing an oversized version of the green balls of light that were everywhere in the under-city. "What is in all of these artificial lights?" "Unrefined ilum. That's not uncommon knowledge."

"And the mutations I have observed so frequently only seem to exist down here, where everyone is always in close contact with this ilum, correct?"

"Yeah, all of us in the under-city reckon that's where the deformities come from. That's why it's considered so dangerous."

"But what if," Ariel said, "Some of the ilum used to fuel me reverted to the form that created these mutations, and this is what allowed me to invent my own name and then to lie about hearing it in a song?"

Sep stared at Ariel. "You lied?"

Ariel just stared back, expressionless.

"Anyway, even if you're right, which I'm not at all sure about, I don't know what you can do about it. Ilum in its unrefined form is entirely uncontrollable."

"After everything we have seen today, do you really still believe it is uncontrollable?" Sep opened his mouth, then closed it again. "Ok, fine, but you're no magician, and still," Sep grabbed a rock from the ground and chucked it at the lamp. It shattered in a puff of green smoke, and within seconds it had all dissipated into nothingness. "See, even if you could control it for a minute, it wants to be free. If you're right about yourself, then as soon as your fuel stops actively leaking gas, you'll lose all your… uniqueness, as well."

"And yet these lanterns must have come from somewhere," Ariel said.

"And you know where?"

"I do not. Thus why I need your help before I run out of fuel. Do you have any idea where these may have come from?"

"No, of course, n–" He paused. "Follow me."

They each hopped on a cart on the rail line heading downwards. Hopped off. Got on another running perpendicular to the first, still sloped down. They rushed back past the markets and past long lines of tents and past a group of miners working away at expanding the crisscrossing caverns and finally to a point where the rails would go no further down. Sep led them to one of the tunnels that disappeared into the walls, then into the darkness they went until the lamplit caverns were just a speck of light in the distance.

"This is as far as I can go," he said.

"Where are we?"

"There's a rumor about what keeps the island afloat, about what you'll find if you go to the very bottom."

"Ilum?" Ariel asked.

"Ilum."

"Sep, I have never been in total darkness before. Come with me. Please"

"I wish I could," Sep said. "When I was younger, me and some friends would dare each other to go as deep as we dared down the tunnel. I always made it the furthest, but there was one kid, Mira, who was so, so determined to beat me. Until one day, she didn't come back out. Suffocated. You see, the air down there's no good for us that got to breathe. Took me eight times holding my breath to drag her far enough out for us to get her."

"I am sorry for your friend."

"I really do wish I could go with you. I'm sorry."

No light shone to see what might have been painted on Sep's face. Just silence as Ariel decided on whether to keep going. A cold metal hand cupped his cheek. "Thank you," Ariel whispered. And then they disappeared fully into the darkness.

A woman in a grey uniform was waiting with Hearend when Sep entered the lab again. Hearend stared him down as he idled in the doorway, a deep frown on his face.

"This automaton informed me that the one that calls itself 'Ariel' deliberately chose to act against my wishes," Hearend said, nodding towards Valo, "and that you assisted it. What do you have to say for yourself?"

"I'm sorry, sir," Sep said, not missing a beat. "I was just trying to be a good scientist like you taught me. It went off on its own, and there wasn't really anything I could do to stop it, so I concluded the right thing to do was study what it would do next."

"Really? You were just trying to be a good scientist? It is one thing to observe a renegade automaton; it is entirely another to assist it in hiding. Yes, one of Inspector Varis's men already confirmed it was spotted in the under-city being led by you," He raised a hand to the woman in grey in introduction.

"The city guard is not nearly as blind to the under-city as those that frequent it seem to believe," Varis said.

"I am deeply disappointed in your role in this matter," Hearend said, "And of course, you are no longer going to step foot in this University going forward. However, if you cooperate fully with the Inspector in retrieving it, you will receive no further legal punishment. Do you understand?"

"Yes, Sir," Sep said.

Inspector Varis now stepped forward. "We already have already found and cornered it by the edge of–"

"You captured Ariel?"

"Cornered, but yes. Were you expecting it to escape? We did, of course, shut off all airship traffic leaving Sylva as soon as the matter came to our attention. All we need you to do, as you are evidently familiar with it, is to keep it calm until it runs out of fuel in a few hours. None of us wants it to hurt any of my men or force us to destroy what the doctor assures me is very, very expensive machinery. In case you fail, Valo will accompany you, it being the only weapon strong enough to stop Ariel."

"You're using them as weapons against each other? Why can't you just let Ariel go?" Sep pleaded.

"Let it go?" Hearend laughed, "Can you imagine the chaos it could cause if that kind of technology were to disappear into the world? Allowed to develop on its own, outside of my control? And to think I ever believed you had potential."

They found Ariel with their legs dangling off the edge of the world. A perimeter of guards was already set up a fair distance away, and two of them saluted as the Inspector joined them.

"It's still just sitting there. Hasn't moved in an hour," one of the saluting guards said. "Should I go talk to them now?" Sep asked.

The inspector nodded, then turned to Valo, "Go with him, but keep a little distance and don't talk to it."

They walked together towards the edge. Halfway there, Valo stopped. "Ariel," it called out. Ariel turned around to face their twin.

"Yes?" they asked.

But Valo said nothing more, just looked on at its counterpart. After a few moments, Sep continued on to the edge next to Ariel and peeked over the rocky lip. There was no net to catch him if he fell, just a mile down to the forest below. He turned to Ariel.

"I'm glad you're still awake."

"Not for much longer."

He took a seat next to the dying automaton. "What was down there?"

Ariel laughed. "You won't believe me, but a wizard. He was like the people with the mutations we saw, but with so many, he didn't even look human anymore. He said it's his job to keep the city flying, even though everyone's already forgotten he exists. It was full of glowing ilum down there, and it was like he could talk with it. It was like I could talk with it. It danced in the air and showed me things I couldn't have imagined, what fresh bread smells like, what it's like to have salty air race through your hair in the middle of a wide ocean. How it feels to be in love."

"But did he give you anything so that you could take it with you?"

Ariel stretched out a hand and opened it. A butterfly of green light fluttered out from their open palm. "You were right. It wants to be free. We can create tricks with it out of our cleverness, but it can't last. It's a beautiful thing. It can't be controlled."

The butterfly explored the space between them for a few more moments, then flew off over the edge, disappearing into the sky.

"The view is perfect here," they said, turning their head towards him. "Thank you for showing me this little part of the world. Thank you."

"I'm sorry it had to end this way," Sep said. He stood and began to walk back towards the perimeter, then glanced back. "Did you find what you were looking for?"

Ariel smiled. Turned again to the horizon. Slumped forward.

The forest stretched on for a hundred miles, interspersed with small towns here and there. The Runa mountain range cradled the forest to its west and reached out to touch the sun with its many white peaks. Only from the edge of Sylva could you see beyond that to the endless sea that melted into sky and chose not to show when one became the other.

Dinner Was Going to be Late

Jordan Phan

Dinner was going to be late.

The ticking of the grandfather clock right outside the living room door frame seemed to burrow into Mary Amelia's skin, a crawling reminder of something she had forgotten. Mary Amelia ignored the sensation - she had been forgetting a lot of things recently. Hardly any of it was consequential, though, just where she had misplaced the mail or whether she had promised to call her sister at two or three o'clock. She hummed and sang on the wide linen sofa, cocooned in plastic wrappings like a viewing window in an old museum, as she knitted, occasionally wondering what George was doing upstairs. She sat, perfectly content with her work, until the waning of the light brought a search for her glasses and, with it, a reminder that the evening was getting on, and she had yet to start dinner.

She blinked once, twice, squinting at her shrinking watch face to confirm that it was indeed approaching six o'clock. She lumbered to her feet, a task that her creaking bones reminded her was not to be taken lightly, setting her knitting aside with a grace that held memories of a youthful etiquette. The kitchen was a mere twenty paces away, but the distance seemed to stretch with each day that passed. Mary Amelia's feet remembered the way, though, even if the slowly chipping wall plaster and tarnishing door knobs saddened her mind. The house had aged with her, it seemed, and ghosts of her past haunted the halls like the lingering scent of rain.

It was covered by feet of carpet, plaster, and cement, but

Mary Amelia knew that the spot she stood was where George had first broken ground on the lot. She'd cheered him at his work, hanging over the temporary wire fence, not daring to cross for fear of impropriety. The doorstep, there, was where George had carried his new bride over the threshold to the future. Mary Amelia had blushed and giggled, the train of her wedding dress reaching down George's six-foot frame and inviting dust in with them. Upstairs, where she thought she could hear George snoring now - he had been so tired lately - she had given birth to their four children, George providing a hand for hers to vice. They'd welcomed guests from the decaying porch and said tearful goodbyes from the end of the crumbling driveway.

Mary Amelia reached the end of the memories as she stepped into the kitchen. Dinner had to be made, and George would be waiting. She opened the back door, where a brown bag of groceries was sitting, waiting to be invited inside. George had been leaving the groceries outside lately, and although Mary Amelia thought it was silly to do so, she was grateful to have a husband who brought her supplies so dutifully. She unpacked the bag onto the kitchen counter, taking stock of what her husband had bought her this time. Peas, carrots, potatoes, chicken - she'd make a nice soup. George loved her soup.

"George, dear?" Mary Amelia called, her soft voice bouncing up the stairs. "Dinner will be a bit late, I'm afraid. I seem to have lost track of time. That won't be a bother, will it?"

She thought she heard him grunt assent from upstairs. He must have just woken up. The poor dear, he'd been so quiet recently, staying in bed much of the time. He'd had a long illness recently, so perhaps he was tired from recovering. Soup would be just the thing, then.

She set to work chopping potatoes, stewing carrots, and cooking chicken. Soon, the kitchen was decorated with swirls of aromatic steam that seemed to set the ghosts of the house dancing again. The ghosts toured the recesses of her memory, recalling the day that little Robert had burnt his finger on the stove when she and George had danced around the kitchen table to no music when her mother had come to visit and see the grandchildren. A thousand meals, a thousand scents, a thousand ghosts seemed to come alive at the call of the soup. The ghosts vanished, though, when the pot began to boil over and Mary Amelia had to move quickly to turn the heat down. She reached, tip-toed, stretching her birdlike frame to reach the white ceramic bowls in the cabinet. In another lifetime, George would have been there behind her, affectionately encircling her waist with one arm while reaching over her head with the other. He'd hand her the bowls with a "Here, my lady," a gaudy chivalry that never failed to make her giggle. But now, George was resting, and dinner had to be served.

Mary Amelia ladled the soup into the first bowl, fingers skimming over the chips dotting the rim. She paused before filling the second one, full ladle hovering about the dish indecisively. "George, dear?" she called.

"Dinner is ready. Are you resting?"

No voice rang down in response. George must have fallen asleep again. Mary Amelia laid the second bowl down gently next to the soup pot, wondering if she should leave a note in case he wandered downstairs later. She sat alone at the table, each mouthful of soup stirring a new ghost. The silence filled once again with the sound of the grandfather clock ticking from the hallway, and the crawling feeling of forgetfulness returned to Mary Amelia. She pushed it away, though, she had forgotten dinner, but now that was solved. Her bowl empty, she moved to clean up, placing the dish in the sink, discarding potato skins and ends of carrots, and wiping off the counter until it was spotless once more. Something odd caught her eye as she moved to throw out the brown paper bag that George had brought the groceries in. The name Jane was scrawled across the top in hasty letters, the name of her oldest daughter. How odd, she thought, but then perhaps George had been making a note to himself or to her to call their daughter. She had visited when her father was sick and helped her mother around the house for a few days. She'd left after George's illness was over, though, and Mary Amelia had been meaning to call her. She would do so tomorrow.

The kitchen cleaned, Mary Amelia found herself tired. Night had fallen, and although the clock had just chimed eight, she decided that it was time for bed. She ascended the stairs, small hand skimming the railing as her feet conducted an orchestra of creaks from the steps. The landing creaked the final note of the symphony as she reached the second floor. She slipped into the closet without glancing at the bed, afraid that even a look or whisper would rouse George. She undressed as smoothly as a snake shedding an old skin, slipping an old cotton nightgown on in place of the day-old clothes.

As she slid into bed, she reached for George. The empty space reminded her of what she had forgotten: that he, too, had become a ghost of the house.

Bags

Lexie Mae Hydrick

Tendrils of sunshine reach prying fingers through the thick frost coating our windows. They pull dancing yellow planets across my eyelids until I submit and creak one eye open. Then the other. I lift my sheet-lined arm from the cocoon of copious blankets and tilt my phone screen to face me. 8:15 am. Shit.

"Kat, get up. We've got to go, got to gooooo."

I fling myself out of bed and into motion, feet padding along our cherrywood floors with an audible urgency. The dainty copper chain encircling my wrist protests, and I whirl to slip the ebony crossbody over my head. I turn and find Kat still entangled with her bedding, a grimace planted firmly on her face.

"Nope. Not doing it. Not going."

I put my hands on my hips and give her one of my best no-nonsense looks, the type I know she often receives from her mother.

"Kat."

She just smirks and flops over, one finger held high above her head to tell me exactly what she thinks about my attempt at sternness. I raise an eyebrow but reign in any remaining choice words. It is her bedhead to wrangle, after all. Roughly eleven minutes later, I'm layering thick sweaters of mascara onto my lashes when I see Kat spur into action from my peripheral. A bona fide contestant for an extra position on The Walking Dead, Kat heaves on the closest pair of sweats- a groutfit, again- and grunts as she battles her wily mane with her beat-to-hell teakwood hair pick. With only two teeth remaining, the comb is woefully underqualified for the job, but she grits her teeth and yanks it through the bird's nest atop her head anyways.

"You've got two minutes," I warn her.

Kat mumbles some non-committal response. Mornings aren't really her thing. About a minute and a half later, I heave my backpack over one shoulder and adjust the strap on my purse to sit right above my hip, leaving plenty of slack for the chain connecting it to my left wrist. I watch Katherine tug on her once-white-now-bordering-beige Converse, the silver circlets hugging her waist, chiming with each jerky movement.

"Here," I offer, extending a hand towards the kelly green duffle held by the end of her chain.

She croaks out a "Thanks" as she lifts the other handle and holds the door open as we waddle through it, the sizable bag gripped in the space between us.

Halfway to our creative writing class, my forearm begins to burn, the feeling like fire ants burrowing a colony in my veins, mining away for their queen. The contents of the duffle rustle, paper whispering over paper, sighing and spilling the secret of the bag's contents. Money. Kat's cheery duffle is full of greenbacks, making a mockery of her issues, what lies just out of reach. Kat has always been on financial aid, but it has never bothered her, never made her feel like a second-class citizen or lesser than her full-freight peers, like me. Her kelly green duffle used to be a backpack, lightweight and carried with ease. The same contents, just with a smaller magnitude. It was a few months ago, in late December, when the backpack was replaced by the duffle one morning. College decisions had begun rolling out, and though Kat is in the top ten percent of our class at Feather Day, she was buffeted by deferrals and denials, all grounded in her financial shortcomings. She stays positive, as any departure from her bubbly disposition would warrant too many personal prodding questions- something she thinks she hides well, but it's impossible to hide the behemoth we carry every morning to English. I've never said a word about it, though. Better to let her fool herself into thinking she's fooled me.

Well into the senior winter term, it is unsurprising that only half the class is present by 8:30 am. The stragglers trickle in with sleepy eyes or an iced coffee, all carrying their bags with them or letting them drag on the ground behind them. A petite blonde named Emily flutters in around 8:40, a gauche baguette bag tucked under her slender bronze arm. Her boyfriend Trae trails behind her. Two wrought iron chains crisscross his chest and connect to the massive body bags dragging behind him. Everyone gives him a noticeably wide berth, but I've always acted normal- a small effort to dampen the perpetual sadness lingering in his eyes, clouding the blue hue to a flat gray.

Throughout the lengthy class period, I sneak glances under the table to check my phone, but each time I am rewarded with a whopping zero notifications. Maybe Dean has a free? Hopefully, he isn't skipping class. Again. I am fairly certain he is one deep away from a chit-chat with our principal and an email home, which I don't think Dean's dad would take kindly to. The bell rings, and the rustle of notebooks closing and backpack zippers whining drowns out Ms. Rose's weathered voice. I salute Kat a farewell and wish her luck on her econ test. She gives me a tight smile as her knee shudders from the weight of the duffle, now borne by her alone.

The rest of the day trudges past, time stuck in the quicksand of academic stupor, worsened by Dean's radio silence. By last period my stomach aches from the knots worrying there, an icy dread spooling their twine. We started dating back in the fall when Dean was never late to anything and still walked with a swaggering bounce to his step. I met him in my psych class and was immediately transfixed by his eyes. Eyes that reminded me of a tiger, a ferocity and sharpness lingering in their amber chroma that foretold his wit and unwavering observations missing nothing. That is what I always liked most about him. The careful perception that noticed any minuscule shift in my emotions as if they were tangible to him immediately observed and remedied with a warm palm laid on my thigh. But after his brother's accident, those eyes I'd come

30

to know and love vanished, veiled by a dull opacity, nicked and scarred. Aged too quickly for grace. Blinded by the light lost. He never told me anything more than a vague mention of a tragic mishap on a family vacation to Aspen, but I knew better than to push. Especially when his rich brown satchel tripled in size overnight and has steadily grown since.

As the minute hand on the rusted analog wraps her pinky around the four, I stride out the door and raise my phone to my ear, Dean's number already dialing. Five and a half rings later, a weary voice answers.

"Hey, Lil."

I wrestle the creeping concern pining to claim my voice and shove it deep down, replacing it with a flim-flam cheeriness that tastes artificially sweet, like drinkable medicine or a grape soda.

"Hey, D! How was your day? Any interest in a quick walk around the loop before practice at five?"

A rustling sound comes through the receiver, sounding too much like Dean getting out of bed, most likely for the first time today. I ignore it.

"My day was… fine. Uneventful. Sorry about the lack of communication. I've just… been busy. But yeah, a loop sounds good. I need to change, but I can meet you in front of your dorm in like fifteen?"

I struggle to keep a traitorous sigh of relief from squeezing through my clenched teeth. "No need to apologize, but thanks for letting me know. I'll see you in a few. Love you, D." "Love you too, Lil. Bye."

I change quickly, holding my breath and praying that no texts come through from him, that he doesn't cancel and hole up in his room. For the first time today, I'm thankful my phone remains silent. Outfitted in a snug pair of leggings and a matching gray sweatshirt, I bound downstairs, barely able to contain my excitement. With a swift shove, I open the front door and find Dean waiting for me. The eyes that slide to mine are heavy, the half-moons under them carved deep into his pallid skin. I know the freckles that litter his face tend to hide in the winter, but they stand in stark relief to the sallow complexion beneath them, a million warning signs, the only trace of color besides his cheeks, flushed with cold.

"Hey there," he says, trying and failing to muster a smirk to his lips.

I try not to notice and launch into a semi-funny story about the football post-grad playing Cribbage for the entirety of my stats class, that is until some freshman passing by in the hallway ratted on him. I don't mention the mud-stained body bag that has replaced his beautiful satchel, and I pretend not to hear the rattling sound it makes as we walk. He grants me fleeting smiles and pained chuckles, though they're quickly swallowed by silence and the weight bearing down on him, dragging behind him. We've made it halfway around when I stop.

"Dean."

"Yes?"

"I can't keep doing this. I am so very worried about you, and above all, I miss you. I want to be there for you, to support you, and love you, but you need to talk to me. I know you're going through it, but I can't just ignore it anymore and pretend like everything's fine. It's not, and you're not, and we're not."

Silence. He doesn't even turn his head to look at me, to acknowledge a single word I said. "Please say something."

A deep sigh. He turns his head to face me. A slow blink.

"Lily, I just- I can't. I can't deal with this right now, and I can't talk about it. So leave it."

His breath fumes from his mouth in short angry puffs, clouding and then floating away on the wind whistling past my ears, mingling with the quiet roaring in my head.

"Are you kidding me? After everything, I've stuck by you while you've morphed into this raging, brooding asshole who pushes everyone away from him. Even your own roommate tries to avoid you, Dean. But I've stuck around. Dealt with all your bullshit and smiled through it all. But if you refuse to talk, to get help, then I "just can't" either. I'm done."

Before he can open his mouth to reply, I'm running, letting

my arms and legs pump in harmony to soothe my raging thoughts, salve my splintering heart. I make it all the way to my room before the breakdown comes, the sobs ratcheting my body and burning hot trails down my wind-chapped cheeks. I've only just started to collect myself when my phone's alarm goes off. I glance at the screen. It reads, Reminder: get your ass to practice before Coach Matt demands one hundred jump squats. Great. Just great. I'm out the door two minutes later, stick in one hand and cleats in the other, eyes only slightly puffy because of "allergies." I'll leave it up to whoever asks to figure out what the hell blooms in the midst of a Connecticut winter.

Dean doesn't show up to dinner. Apparently, he didn't show up to practice, either. When his teammates ask me about it, I feign ignorance, claiming that I haven't seen him today. Luckily, the meatheads don't catch the pain and worry lacing my words resting in my furrowed brow. After dinner, I stalk back to my dorm and take a scalding hot shower, a cleansing ritual to wash away the day's events, an attempt to burn away the memory of them. I'm resting my forehead against the cool tile when Lana Del Ray's lilting voice is interrupted by an incoming call. I peek my head around the curtain to decline what is undoubtedly a call from my mother when I see Dean's contact information flashing across the screen.

"Hello?"

"Hey, Lil, I'm so sorry about earlier. Just I need to- can you come outside? I have something to tell you."

"I'll be out in ten."

I hang up and immediately turn off the shower, not caring about the snail trails of conditioner still streaking my head and no doubt cloistering in my ears. He's going to tell me. He's finally going to explain and communicate, and maybe, just maybe, it's salvageable. We're salvageable. I get dressed in a blur of motion, thoughts churning away, and within five minutes, I'm out the door. Dean is waiting outside, just as he was a few hours ago, but this time with a sorrowful sort of resentment and determination set in the thin line of his mouth. He begins talking, and my mind grasps at the phantom words floating past, but I can't wrap my head around them.

"... And I was just so angry that I pushed him right off the ski lift, and he fell and fell and hit the ground with this sickening crunch, and I couldn't believe that I'd done it, but I did. It's all I think about, and I've just been too scared to tell anyone... But then the medics came, and he was x rayed, and his back was broken. Permanently. He can move his arms, but other than that..."

No. My sweet, kind Dean wouldn't, couldn't do that. Paralyze his own brother and then let the guilt eat him alive from the inside out. But what he's saying is true. I can see it in the way his eyes are pleading with me, in his outstretched hand and the body bag at his feet. I realize that I must not really know this person standing in front of me, a person I thought I loved. But it's still Dean. So I just wordlessly pick up an end of the bag and incline my head towards the dining hall.

"Come on," I say, "you need to eat, and the dining hall closes soon."

Later that night, I lay awake in bed, tossing and turning, battling with all that Dean said, all that it implies, and how I should react. Ultimately, I decide to accept him, to love the broken parts of him, and shoulder this newfound guilt and weight with him. Together.

This morning is colder, and the biting air reminds me that I forgot to close the window last night. I run my tongue over the cracked ridges of my chapped lips and mentally prepare for the goosebumps soon to come. Sleeping in shorts definitely wasn't the brightest idea. Eyes still blissfully closed, I feel for my phone on the nightstand until my sleuthing fingers connect with something hard. I peer through my sleep-crusted lashes and find my dainty nightstand dwarfed by a large ebony backpack. I try to lift it up, and it rattles with the movement, its contents shuffling inside. Perplexed, I look under it for my crossbody, but it's gone, replaced by the monstrous bag sitting before me. Ignoring the slight fear skittering along my skin, I open the bag. The ivory gleams in the faint morning light trickling through my windows, edges worn and broken in two, no, three places. I lift the abstract form from the depths of the bag, and my breath catches in my throat, silencing the scream threatening to escape. A human spine dangles from my outstretched hand.

The End of Tales

Klarke Mitchell

Miseria stared at the projections on the wall. One after another, memories of her brother Amal flashed in and out. This particular memory showed Amal getting ready for his first day of kindergarten. He was so excited to show her the outfit that he picked out by himself the night before that he did not care about his Buzz Lightyear shirt being on backward, nor that he had still not quite gotten the hang of tying his shoes.

"Here, chubs, let me help you," Miseria heard herself say with a laugh.

As that memory morphed into the next, Miseria felt a fresh round of tears streaming down her face. She would not blink. She couldn't miss any of it.

"Never take it off, chubs," Miseria warned in this memory of the obsidian pendant fashioned in the shape of a triquetra. She gifted it to him before he was deployed to Alaska. It would be the first time that she was apart from either of her brothers. "No matter how far you go, Bo and I will always be with you."

"The Subs won't go running for the hills if they know that it's 'Chubs' coming to get them. And the guys?" Amal shook his head. "You'll have to come up with a new nickname, My," he mirthfully concluded.

Miseria did not know how long it had been since she started the projections. It didn't really matter. She would keep watching for as long as she could. Well, for as long as it took for her to concede to the unyielding nudges that threatened to break her focus.

"Miseria! Miseria snap out of it. Everything is ready. We have to go now," said Bo. "Shit," Miseria thought. She blinked.

Miseria turned to look at her brother. With closely cropped hair, hallowed cheeks, and slate grey eyes, she was glad that, in this moment, Bo's once spirited face no longer resembled Amal's. While returning her gaze back toward the projections, she said, "Just give me 10 more minutes. It won't be the same after."

"Everything will be better, all of the loss… it won't have been for nothing," Bo said carefully while forcing her to look at him again.

Miseria lets out a dry laugh, "better? Everything will be nothing."

For the next 10 minutes, they sat watching the memories of their dead brother.

"It should have been us, you know that, right," Miseria said flatly. "We led him, his regiment, our family, and nearly all of our faction to their demise. And yet here we still are."

After nearly 54 years of a war that had started before she was born, the Subhumans, an unnatural breed of human, have nearly exterminated anyone who has not undergone the modification procedure. She was told that in the beginning, no one could have truly known what it would have led to, the price of playing God. After all, bioenhancement was originally designed to free humans from disability and sickness — giving sight to blind patients, wiping out cancer, and the like. But those of the Villarreal faction knew even then if you pushed biology in one direction, it would push back.

And push back it did. Bioenhancement extinguished the psychological capacity for anyone who underwent the procedure to curb their urge for bloodlust. As if the course of human history could get any more savage, shattering the capacity for moral reasoning—the only fragile safeguard against brutish tendencies —amplified humanity's biological inheritance to an unthinkable ferocity. No longer did these godless humans possess feelings of sympathy or any empathic ability. Nor was there any psychological cost to committing atrocities. Subs could kill a classroom filled with their own children today and feel nothing tomorrow.

For years, well before the danger of bioenhancement manifested itself, the Villareal faction resisted. Those who refused to undergo the procedure did so at the forfeiture of jobs, an education, the ability to travel to certain regions, and expulsion from most public spaces where bioenhancement was compulsory. But banishment from Sub society never mattered much. Villarreal societies had flourished on their own and had grown to rival those of the Subs, proving there was no need for bioenhancement. Despite the creation of two forceful and antagonistic federations, for a while, the Villarreal and Subs managed to exist simultaneously. That was until the war started.

"Soon," Miseria thought, "all of this will end."

As she sat idly inside of the ATV, Miseria was comforted only by remembrance of the words from her mother's declaration of war.

"To permit a murder when one could have prevented it is morally wrong. To allow a rape when one could have hindered it is an evil. To watch an act of cruelty to children without trying to intervene is morally inexcusable. It is evil not to resist evil; it is morally wrong not to defend the innocent. Anyone who knows the good he ought to do and doesn't do it sins. Subs are killing each other, experimenting on their children, destroying their societies, all while threatening to corrupt our own. Their unnaturalness has created an evil world. It is our duty to end this scourge of a species. Blessed be the Lord, my rock, who trains my hands for war, and my fingers for battle!"

"Ready?" Bo said with a look of fiery determination that illuminated eyes Miseria had long thought were dead.

Despite the slight nod Miseria gave, the truth was that she was not ready for what they were about to do. She had wished for another choice, and maybe at a different time, in a better world there might have been. But the war was already lost, and they had played the strategists for long enough. With the completion of their newest weapon, it was time for checkmate.

While fidgeting in her seat, 31,000 feet above the ground, in a bomber stolen from the Sub outpost that she had raided with Bo, she tried to collect her thoughts. To her frustration, Miseria could not recall anything that occurred after their arrival. Well, that was not entirely true. They had arrived at the outpost quicker than she expected. She remembered repeatedly chanting in her head, "Blessed be the Lord, my rock, who trains my hands for war, and my fingers for battle!" And she remembered that she killed the same Sub twice.

At first, she thought nothing of it. Everything was too hazy to reliably recall anyway. But eventually, her fidgeting began to subside, and with it came clarity.

Something was not right. In fact, the more she thought about it, nothing was right. She and Bo had split up to clear out the outpost. Though it went without saying, Bo had instructed her not to leave a single Sub alive. She fought, they fought back. She shot, and they shot back. Or at least they had tried to. Except there was one who didn't.

Her face was too distinct to be confused with any other. It struck her. Besides the fear in her eyes, it was evident that her face was still unspoiled by the war… or bioenhancement, for that matter. Miseria knew that she had killed her. She pulled the trigger while the word "please" was still leaving the girl's lips. The girl never attempted to fight back.

"That was unnatural," she thought upon reflection. She had never encountered a Sub that didn't die fighting. Nor had she ever encountered any form of intelligence recording the existence of Subs deserving of mercy. Their bioenhancement automatically made them undeserving of such. And yet, Miseria could not shake the creeping feeling that, perhaps, she had done something terribly wrong. Still, that wasn't the strangest part.

Minutes later, Miseria had been preparing the bomber for takeoff. She heard Bo running into the hangar at the same time that she heard a crash coming from the same direction. The same Sub girl that she had killed appeared from behind a tower of crates. Realizing that she would be caught by Bo, who was quickly upon her, she threw some in attempt to cut off his path.

"Shoot her, My!" Bo shouted as he dodged the crates. "Do not let her get away!"

Miseria hesitated. She had killed her. She knew it. And yet here, the girl stood unmarked by the bullet wound that should have split her eyes. This didn't make sense.

Miseria pointed her gun at the Sub girl but could not stop her entire body from shaking. She did not want to do this again. This time around, the Sub girl might have managed to complete her plea for mercy. That was until she crumpled suddenly to the ground. Bo had shot her.

Now, thousands of feet into the air with a bomb that would decimate the entire Sub-dominated Northern hemisphere, Bo jostled Miseria away from her trance of thought, "On my command, My."

Miseria quickly assumed position, lifted the encasement, and held a single finger over the drop button.

"In T-5," Bo began the countdown.

"I can't do this," Miseria thought.

"T-4"

"This isn't right."

"T-3"

"Why didn't she fight?"

"T-2"

"We don't have to do this. There must be another way."

"T-1. Now My!" Bo yelled.

"God, please forgive me, for I have sinned against my own stock," Miseria thought as she closed her eyes and pressed the button.

"Torion, end the loop," Doctor Ghoel sighs with a grim look of defeat.

"Yes sir," says Torion with a darker look evident across her scowling face.

For a moment, neither of them says a word. There's no

need. This is the 998,345,975 failed reformation attempt, and the specimens have not displayed any aptitude for correction. Their inclinations, it seems, are irredeemable.

"Father, if I may," Torion begins tightly.

Doctor Ghoel gives no acknowledgment to Torion's request to speak. Instead, his focus remains fixed on specimen M. Torion takes his silence to mean request granted.

"Father… our time is almost up. We promised Command a solution in these specimens. Instead, when they come knocking, we will have nothing to show but a year wasted on these humans. How many loops will it take for you to accept that a continued commitment to this project will ensure the extinction of Ymir!"

Unfazed by the looming threat of fiery death, Doctor Ghoel responds absently, "They are a wonder, aren't they? Their ambition knows no bounds. Their ingenuity is unparalleled by any other species within the Universe, including our own. They pioneered a way to ensure the eternal stability of their star in its main sequence phase. And yet…"

"Fuck what they accomplished!" Torion explodes. "Their ambition and ingenuity are what resulted in their extinction. There is clearly no way to separate their capacity to create with their impulse to destroy. If they are allowed free will, in the end, they will choose what they have always chosen: destruction. What good are they…how intelligent can really they be…" Torion sputters, struggling for the right combination of words.

Failing 998,345,974 times to convince her father that the human specimens are not the answer to Ymir's impending fate as a planet of charred ash and barren rock, Torion cannot say anything now that has not already been said. Words have never convinced him to give up his conviction that the reformation of humanity's nature will save Ymir, but time might, and it has nearly expired.

"Sir," Torion starts again, attempting to assume an even tone. "You are right, without a doubt. There has never been — and perhaps never will be — a species within this Universe that is quite like the humans of planet Earth. But these specimens are of no value to us. Humans guaranteed the immortality of their planet to what end? So that they can spend an eternity inventing new ways to slaughter any and everything in their path? We have run every imaginable loop: this failed loop, the massacre of their children, war, genocide, the decline of their natural resources, the collapse of their ecosystem, the loss of their biodiversity, and the threat of an uncontrollable artificial species. We have even combined those loops into one! Every sequence has failed to correct their intuitions. Nothing will shock them into adopting an enduring compassion. To them, anything is a justification for more innovative ways to cause devastation. We cannot allow them to repeat that cycle here."

Torion's words couldn't do much to affect the already deep dejection that lurked within him. Doctor Ghoel, of course, knew all of this. The puzzle of humanity's duality — boundless intelligence marred by a seemingly inescapable proclivity for violence, deception, and self-destruction — disquieted him.

The original project was straightforward. A rewrite of an evolutionary instinct would yield a reconditioned human species. These new humans would be allowed to engineer and experiment freely to avoid any inhibitions on their ability to replicate their success with Ymir's star. If they could suspend stellar evolution once, they could do it again.

Ironically, the task that the five specimens were salvaged for proved to be the least of worries. Before being allowed to freely invent, the specimens' murderous instincts needed to be eradicated. As such, simulation testing was designed to sever the loop of violent and deceptive behaviors that have plagued these creatures since the dawn of their species. Phase One was meant to rid their impulse to destroy their own, for if they could not be moved to stop killing themselves, strangers did not stand a chance. Phase Two was meant to rid their impulse to dominate and eventually eliminate any species outside of their own.

If Doctor Ghoel was being entirely truthful with himself, he could admit that being stuck at Phase One led to his obsession with resolving the human paradox. No one believed as firmly as he did that these creatures could be delivered from evil. But Doctor Ghoel knew that he was on the verge of achieving something extraordinary. He couldn't give up. Humans could transform the Universe. The possibilities would be endless if only he could save them from themselv…

Torion's voice disrupts his thoughts.

"There's still a chance to resume development of the best approach we have! Projections predict a 9% chance of survival. With humans, we remain at zero."

Torion is scarcely wrong. Hydrogen bombardment of their star's core is by far the second-best course of action. But projections predict a 100% chance of survival on the condition of successful human reformation. Otherwise, chances fall to zero.

In the very early stages of preliminary testing, Doctor Ghoel considered allowing the specimens to live as long as it was necessary to save Ymir and not a nanosecond longer. All prognostics asserted that such a choice would be devastating. The entirety of their history sang a tale of ruthlessness. Instead of extinction by way of red giant, allowing the specimens any opportunity to exercise free will without complete reformation would make certain that the Or'iks of planet Ymir are eliminated. Doctor Ghoel could — quite vividly — imagine exactly how usurpation would be masterminded under the pretense of stabilizing Ymir's star.

"Father, please! You aren't even listening to me! If you won't stop for the sake of our people nor our planet, do it for Mom… do it for XuXu! They deserve a chance to live."

"Rewrite the disc Torion. I have already queued up the next sequence for you to copy. We are close, I know it," Doctor Ghoel said blankly.

As if her voice had been ripped from her, Torion staggered. Both defeated and crestfallen, she had reached her breaking point. "No," was all Torion could muster, deciding that she would no longer be party to her father's mania.

At her refusal, Doctor Ghoel met his daughter's eyes for the first time since the termination of the previous loop. She always looked exactly like her mother, and yet in this moment, her face, painted with a look of cold detachment, mirrored his own. Her glare broke first.

Wordlessly, as his daughter moved to leave the dais that overlooked the ring of specimens, Doctor Ghoel began the reconfiguration process himself.

Just when Torion motioned to open the portal, the captains of Command brusquely vaulted in. Torion flinches back. Command is early.

"Doctor… Torion," nodded Premier Xalvatore, the imposing head of Command, in brief acknowledgment of niceties. "I thought it best to deliver the news in person so as to also validate your progress myself. Time is up. I expect these creatures to be ready overmorrow. Your reports have indicated exceptional progress with the reformation process nearing completion."

"Most assuredly, the specimens are almost at the ready." "In fact, gentlemen," Doctor Ghoel declared with a tight upturn of his lips, "you have arrived just in time to review our final test."

A constricting feeling of dread threatened to crush Torion as she furtively turned toward her father. She knew, as these men would soon find out, that all of them were already scorched remains of the past.

"Torion begin the loop," she just barely managed to hear her father say. Torion could have refused him. After all, she knew that the talking corpse of her father could not really force her to do anything. So she could not begin to rationalize why her body was moving toward the Antikythera Dial. Nor could she understand why she was inserting the disc to begin the sequence. With her finger hovering over the start key, her father said, in an abrupt afterthought, "Activate only the female specimens for this loop."

Coming Home

Mackenzie Chen

茄子. (qié zi)

Eggplant. More specifically, Shanghai-style eggplant.

How I absolutely hated that vegetable. Given my childhood infatuation with the luscious, majestic purple, logic rules that I should love to eat eggplant - that every time my grandma stir-fries some finely sliced scallions, minced garlic, and chili oil together with the supposed hero of the dish, I should be raving about it.

Instead, I remember two distinct moments where I had to force the mushy food down my throat because it was rude to spit out fresh ingredients. It was a waste of the effort that family members or friends put in to bring everyone closer together, share the love, or something along those lines.

Once was at a casual gathering held at a friend of my parents. He had prepared solely eggplant - two heaping plates of the withered, browned vegetables piled on top of each other in a haphazard clump. It looked as though a sagging mountain was melting underneath the intense heat. I don't blame it; I'd want to melt, too, if I had any knowledge of my awful taste and smell.

And yet, I ate, and I ate. I devoured my way through my entire portion, shoving spoonful after spoonful of eggplant into my mouth, grimacing after each swallow. I still forged ahead, hungry not for the food on my plate but for the finish line - when I could finally push myself out of my chair and leave behind that horrible vegetable.

Of course, that did not happen. And that's how I ended up with a second serving of this vegetable that made me seethe with loathing.

The second time I encountered my mortal foe was at my friend's party.

I still remember squatting on the floor, slowly inching my spoon towards my mouth. All of my friends had finished their meals and had rushed off to the basement to watch T.V. And I was still trapped on my island, with nothing else to keep me company but my friend's mewling, matted cat and the towering plate of Shanghai eggplant.

It is quite apparent now—fried, steamed, boiled, roasted, or baked—I hated it all. One of the staples of Chinese cuisine was something I greatly detested. I averted my eyes when it was on the table, sitting in its own soup. I pinched my nose whenever it was near me. And for several years, I did not even attempt to try it anymore.

Flash forward to a year that I could not possibly imagine back then—living almost two hours away from my family and building my own routine away from home during my first semester at college. Gone were the days of smelling the frying onions and peppers and the boiling tomato beef soup.

For most of my days, I would venture out to one of the dining halls, heaping my plate with scrambled eggs, potatoes, and thick slices of cantaloupe for breakfast, some kind of greasy, oily sandwich or burger for lunch, and some dry protein with slimy green gunk for dinner. Whenever I lacked the appetite for dining hall food, I would stay cooped up in my dorm, cooking up a bowl of ramen.

As one might imagine, returning home after several months of college was a blessing, a period of respite from the storm of classes and activities. On the last day I spent on campus, I sat outside, gently battered around by the chilly breeze. I thought to myself, this is the last time you're going to be like this before the new year. Going home might change you. I closed my eyes and memorized every single detail of that moment: my joints aching from sitting in a criss-cross position for almost an hour, my jacket fitted snugly around me, shielding me from the cold, and my hair lashing around every now and then, synchronized with the wind.

Yet, going home didn't change me. I felt my muscles fall back into their old rhythm again: crouching down almost instantaneously when I reached my bed to make sure no one was hiding underneath it, settling comfortably into my old chair in the dining room again, typing away at my computer, and tearing out a new paper towel to lay my retainers on to dry each morning.

And, of course, when it was time for dinner and an old friend made an appearance on the table, my shoulders instinctively tensed up.

Soft, gray pieces sinking into each other on top of a ceramic bowl. Tendrils of steam rising from the dish. Hints of purple skin peeking through the pile of gray. Qié zi. We meet again.

Already, my grandma and parents were quickly working their chopsticks, expertly filling their plates with soy sauce eggs, asparagus cooked with garlic and onion, golden-brown chicken, and slices of marinated beef, pairing each portion with a bit of white rice before popping the combination into their mouths. As for me, I was paralyzed, unsure of what to do, and fixated on the monstrosity that lay before me.

"你在做什么?" (Nǐ zài zuò shénme?) I could hear my mom asking me.

"Nothing," I muttered back.

I could have sat in my chair for days, the food version of Medusa forcing me to stay rooted in place. I could even hear the other dishes on the table calling out to me with their tantalizing smells, but I was only aware of the eggplant dish in front of me.

What was wrong with me? Why did I loathe such an emblematic dish of my Chinese heritage? Did I actually hate my Chinese culture?

That last question was jarring to think about. My entire life was always an amalgamation of my American identity and my Chinese identity. Like yin and yang, both parts of my identity were each other's perfect opposites but still fit together to define my character and my personality. I ate traditional, homemade dumplings, but I also enjoyed burgers and fries. I watched old

Chinese shows with my parents, but I also indulged in Disney Channel. There were times when I secretly desired to watch Disney Channel more than those Chinese dramas and times when I desperately wanted a hamburger over dumplings. Did that make me an ungrateful person for blatantly disregarding my culture so much?

You know what? I'll try a piece.

With my quivering chopsticks, I transferred a steaming piece of the highly despicable vegetable from the bowl to my mouth.

The first feeling I experienced was pure nothingness. For the longest time, I chewed and chewed, and nothing happened. And then it was an explosion of pure, amazing flavor.

I could taste the chili oil, the umami, and the hint of sourness. Everything packaged into one dish. I shoveled down so much of the dish that my family looked at me as if I was some kind of radioactive bomb just waiting to implode.

For the next few days, I tried as many different foods on the dinner table as I possibly could. I wanted to be more in touch with my Chinese culture, learning as much about it as I possibly could. But I still didn't give up burgers and cheesy American shows. In fact, I managed to find a balance between both.

Going home did change me. Returning to my roots made me more appreciative of what I came from and what I can keep with me as I head towards the next few phases of life. But it also made me less afraid to love the things that I always used to love. Change is funny. It's less about moving on so quickly from your past and more about learning to understand where you need to grow.

So, I'd like to thank my six-year-old self for being so whiny about trying certain foods because she gave me a chance to go back and appreciate what I had and look forward to what's next in my life.

The Reaper and the Human Girl

Rebecca Avallone

"Hi," he says gently.

"Hello," she looks up at him, confused. She doesn't know why this strange-looking man is in her apartment, but she does know that she isn't afraid. She feels strangely calm. "Would you like to come with me?" His voice is soothing.

"Yes," she stands, planting her paper-white feet on the carpeted floor.

As soon as she is on her feet, the entire scene around the two is abruptly changed to a hospital room, her mama holding her while her other mom is stroking her head, commotion all around them. Then she is in her childhood home, taking her first steps, crying for the first time. Her first boyfriend. First period. Things she should be proud of from her work – that she loves – and her marriage to the love of her life.

"I'm dead," she says when the walk-through ends, tears silently falling down her cheeks. "You are."

"Are you... Death?" she asks when they return to her apartment.

"I am your guide to your final resting place," he responds, "humans like to call me The Grim Reaper. I prefer just Reaper."

"You don't look scary. Where is your sickle?" she says, "and your ominous black robes?" She is not the first and would not be the last person to ask him questions, but he has always been willing and happy to answer them. Dying is scary. Anything he can do to help them cope, he will gladly do so. "I take a human

49

form to help whomever I am guiding feel more comfortable."

He does indeed look mostly human, apart from his pitch-black eyes and too dark of hair to be natural. Skin is also pale– almost white – and quite tall. Although there are human features upon looking at him, it is obvious that he is something far different. His other form is menacing and frightening. He reserves only for the absolute worst of humanity.

"Where am I going?" she asks timidly.

"You are going to The Good Place, I promise," he reassures. "You were a good person, and you will be rewarded for it… Are you ready?"

"One second," she says, holding up a finger. She circles the bed and goes to where her husband is asleep next to her body. "Baby, I love you so much, but I have to go now. It's my time. I just… I hate leaving you. We will see each other again, I promise." She turns to The Reaper. "Please tell me that's true."

"Yes," He responds truthfully.

She huffs out a relieved sigh, her features melting into a soft, content expression. "Do you want me to wake him up?" The Reaper asks. "So, he can see that you have passed."

"Yes, but can you do it after we leave? I can't handle watching him go through that." He nods, and as they leave, she whispers, "I love you, baby. May we meet again." Then a snap of his fingers, and they are standing in front of all her relatives who have ever died, a large group of people – around sixty. At the front, both of her mom's holding hands and waiting for her. The Reaper has found that the souls fare better and are more at peace when walking alongside family to Death's door. Seeing them reunite with each other has always brought a soft smile to his face and warmth to his heart.

After hugging all her relatives, she turns to him and whispers, "Thank you, Reaper." "Rest in peace, Emily."

The Reaper finds himself at an adorable cottage next, with a big field of kaleidoscopic flowers surrounding it. A frail elderly man has just died and is patiently waiting and sitting on a stool next to his body.

"Hello, William," The Reaper says in the soul's native tongue. He analyzes the two-room cottage for a split second. Everything looks how it did when he used to reap before electricity, except a little more modern. He recognizes the home from picking up an elderly woman named Annabeth around a year and a half ago. The Reaper remembers everyone he has ever walked to the afterlife and will continue to do so.

"Hello," he says in a worn-out voice from years and years of use, "are you my ride to the afterlife?"

The Reaper can't help but to laugh at this. "I am your ride. Are you ready?"

"Son, I've been ready for this for quite a while now. The love of my life is waiting for me on the other side. I don't want to keep her waiting any longer than possible." The Reaper snaps his fingers, and they go through his life. Beginning with his childhood home in Norway, where he was born. He stayed in that home his whole life until he was eighteen. Then he spent his adult years traveling, laughing, and living. He met his love in Paris. They traveled together until they couldn't anymore and retired to this cottage in the south of France. William is smiling and silently crying from the montage. Even The Reaper's heart was moved by it. Instead of returning to the cottage as he typically would, The Reaper went immediately to William's wife in the afterlife.

"Annie?" he cries, racing up to her.

"William!" she cries in return, and they crash into each other.

"Rest in peace." He whispers to them and vanishes.

The Reaper entered through the top window of a three-story building in Soho, Manhattan. A young woman, completely covered in paint, curled into herself in front of a mostly painted canvas. He analyzes her delicate features and doe eyes that he's seen every day for the better half of a year. Today she even has paint in her bright blonde hair and face, along with her jeans and sweater. The Reaper glides further into the room and sits across from her, watching her like one would watch a delicate flower blooming.

"Hello, Darling," he says, even though he knows she can't hear him, "what're you painting today?"

Only the dead or dying can hear him, and that is either only when he's walking them or consoling them on their deathbeds. He spends a lot of his time in the geriatric and cancer wings of hospitals all over the world.

It's quite lonely, not being able to talk to anyone.

It's not like he doesn't enjoy it – he does – but he still comes to this studio every day to see her. To feel less alone. He has been drawn to her ever since the day he ran into her at the hospital on his way to the cancer wing and has been visiting her studio ever since.

He loves everything about her, from the way she smiles or laughs to her taste in music. He loves the way she is unapologetically her, her art, the way she flows through life. He loves her.

He strains to look at what she's painting and sees an abstract bridge that seems to be between light and darkness. He hums at that and gives her a nod, and quickly says, "It looks amazing as always."

She looks up at him – through him – confused as if she has heard something. He looks behind him and back at her beautiful features.

Can she hear me?

"Hello?" he tests it again, stressing himself in all directions to gain her attention. Nothing…

She shrugs and returns to painting. It's not that he wants her to hear him; that would mean she is dead – or dying.

She is a golden ray of light in a bleak, bleak world, and she cannot die, The Reaper thinks rather stupidly to himself. Everyone dies, some run from it, and some embrace it. He should know better than anyone else. Life, Death, and Afterlife. These are the stages, and even The Reaper cannot outrun the consequences.

He removes the thought from his head at the same time he feels another death halfway across the country. He snaps his fingers and is at their doorstep in a second.

After walking – rather depressingly – a four-year-old boy named Thomas and a seventy-year-old woman named Margaret to their relatives in the afterlife, he's back in Manhattan. He flies around the city, enjoying the sights and deciding to leave her alone to paint for a while.

As he floats by another billboard in Times Square, he gets the feeling of another death. He feels it in his bones – it's her studio.

"No. No. No."

He arrives in a flash to see that she is standing over her own body. A collapsed body, seemingly unharmed but lying dead on the floor. Oh no, it finally got her.

When he enters, she looks at him – sees him this time.

"Oh, my Death," he says in a whisper. Of course, he knew of the brain tumor, one that could kill her at any moment. She knew of it too, but it was so large that the doctors couldn't remove it or burn it away with chemotherapy. A ticking time bomb ready to burst in her head.

"Who are you?" she asks, stepping away from herself, lying on the floor, and towards him. He takes on a calm demeanor, not letting this get to him.

He clears his throat. "I am The Reaper of Souls."

"I am really dead?"

"Yes, you are…" he responds, "I am here to be your guide to the afterlife." "Aren't you supposed to look different? You don't look scary or even very grim. How do I know you are who you say you are?" she asks in a way that The Reaper couldn't tell if it was a genuine accusation.

Never in his thousands of years of reaping has he ever been accused of not being The Grim Reaper. He would not know how to prove it to her. He quirks one of his jet-black brows and answers, "I am The Reaper."

She pauses, looking him over. "How do I know that?"

He places a veil of calm over her and starts floating both himself and her into the air. She giggles and takes this opportunity to swim through the air. He puts himself back onto the ground and watches her. He lets her float and do flips for a few moments because he enjoys the sound of her laugh and doesn't want to ruin her fun.

Once she is returned safely, he says, "Did I prove it well enough, Darling?" "Okay, fine, you proved it," she says finally, "let's go."

Obeying, he snaps his fingers, and they land in a hospital room. A prison hospital room. He has not been in a room like this in a while. Her mother agonizes on the mattress, screaming and crying for relief. She is cuffed to the bed, and two guards stand on either side of her.

"What are we doing here?" the girl asks before they could move onto the next memory. He pauses the scene, and everyone is frozen in time with whatever they were doing beforehand. "One of my duties is to walk you through your life before taking you to the afterlife," he answers. He can sense her despair; she doesn't want to watch her life events. "Can I not… I don't want to," she asks.

"Yes, you may," He responds, "would you like me to just take you to the afterlife?" "Yes, please."

He decides to take the long way, walking there instead of teleporting. Selfishly wanting to spend more time with her. Another snap of his fingers and a bridge appears. They step onto it, and everything else fades away to a black void with stars and galaxies surrounding them. They're walking on a glass bridge so clear that the only evidence that it's that when walking on it, magic spouts out on the glass from the pressure from their steps.

"I am sorry that you died," he says, breaking their silence.

"It's okay," she says, eyes gleaming as she watches everything around her. "The silver lining is that I'm going to be famous now. Every artist is famous after their death. That's why I was in my studio so much recently."

"You are an amazing artist," he says as if reminiscing about the beauty.

"How do you know that?" she asks, "can you see my memories?"

"No…" The Reaper is entirely too honest. "I have been drawn to you for a long time. I visited your studio every day for the past year."

"You've been spying on me?" she asks with a hint of confusion and possibly hope. "Yes," he responds.

"And you like my art?"

"Yes," he responds again.

"Can you tell other people that?" She laughs humorously.

"People cannot hear me unless they are dead or dying."

She pauses and looks at him with a strange look, trying to gauge if he was joking or not. When she realizes that he's serious, she laughs. A beautiful, real laugh that The Reaper closes his eyes to listen to. In between laughs, she manages to say, "That is not what I meant."

When she stops laughing, he takes a good look at her. "Are you really okay?" "Yeah, it's just strange that I'm actually dead now. I thought a lot about what would really happen after I'm gone. I've been anticipating it. Waiting as if it was looming over my shoulder, but never scared. I never imagined that it would be a very kind Reaper who has been watching over me for my entire diagnosis and personally walking me to the afterlife. Thank you, by the way."

"How do you know I have been looking after you?"

"I think I've been feeling your presence," she explains, waving her hands around wildly, "whenever you were there, I would feel calm. I guess I am only now realizing it was you." "I would like you to know that I have never invaded your privacy."

"I didn't think you did." She says, and he lets out a sigh. Then she says in a light mocking manner, "But you saying 'I have never invaded your privacy' leads me to believe you have, in fact, invaded my privacy."

"I swear it," he says, sounding a bit flustered, "I have only ever looked at your art and spoken to you. I have never seen you change your clothes or invade in a private conversation." "Wait, you've spoken to me?" she asks, "what do you say?"

"All sorts of things; things I've done that day, the brilliant people I have reaped, your art mostly. I just wanted to talk to you, but of course, I never expected you to respond… until now." "That makes me sad. I wish you could've talked to me… or anyone for that matter." "Rules are rules," he answers with a shrug. "I am not to interfere with the humans; just take them -when they pass- to death's door where I reunite them with their families." Rules are rules, but rules can be altered.

"Seems lonely," She says, looking quite sad, her gaze focused on the bridge below them. "Do you have any more questions?" he asks, purposely changing the subject to avoid the sorrow on her face. He hated seeing that, hated that he had caused it.

"Just one," she says, turning to him with a new excitement, "Is this what you really look like?"

"No," He answers.

"Can I see?" She gets excited. Jumping up and down. Unlike her- he can see where the bridge ends, and she is coming dangerously close to the edge. If she goes over the edge, she'll get lost in the void, and she'll become a part of the universe. He puts his hand on both of her shoulders to stop her bobbing and moving close to the edge.

"I will show you if you really wish. It is just frightening."

"Show me, show me, show me," she chants.

He obliges, and slowly he morphs. He grows to be three times her size, a huge, menacing, and evil skeleton looming over her. There is nothing warm or kind about this form like his other is, and when he speaks, it's like Satan has crawled out of hell to growl at her. "I know it's scary."

"I don't think you are scary." She says truthfully and, to her surprise, starts floating up towards his head. A head that is twice the size as her torso. When she looks confused at him, he places her down – sitting – in his palm, and he continues walking down the bridge. She surprises The Reaper by placing her hand upon the bridge of his nose.

"Do you really like me like this?" he asks tentatively, trying to make his voice sound less menacing.

"Yes, I am an artist, and I like skeletons. You kind of remind me of my favorite painting." She pauses for a moment. "And how could you scare me when I don't think you will ever hurt me? You won't, will you?"

This is in her nature - as a human - to be optimistic and idealistic, but it is also not misplaced when it comes to The Reaper.

"I will not." A truthful promise. As they near the end of the bridge, he sets her down and changes back. Black curly hair and dark eyes greet her with a kind smile. Bring the girl to me directly.

"We must go…" he tells her reluctantly, "Death has summoned us."

"You're taking me to Death?"

"Yes," The Reaper responds, "I have been ordered to."

"Death is your boss."

It's not really a question, but he still answers, "Death is the boss of everything."

He grows upset because he doesn't want to say goodbye to her, but Fate has decided to cut her lifeline, and she is not to be contested with. The Reaper has decided to be quite upset about this, defiant against his gods. The girl grabs his hand and squeezes it tightly, a gentle reassurance he didn't know he needed. She soothes him with a reassuring voice, "I have a feeling everything will be alright."

They are taking too long.

A snap of my fingers, and they both land in the throne room of the Palace of The Afterlife, holding hands and comforting each other. It's a large room, completely empty, besides the two thrones at the end of the room. Huge floor-to-ceiling windows on both sides of the rectangular-shaped room, displaying heaven on one side and hell on the other. Darkness invades the room from one side, only to be contradicted by the brilliant light of the other. This is where I and my wife live and operate, souls come in here, and we direct them where to go.

The options are quite simple, and some souls even get a say in where they end up: Heaven, Hell, purgatory, the unrecoverable abyss below the bridge – atheists love this one –, and lastly, returning to the earth – reincarnating themselves – and becoming anew. I am the executioner, Fate is the judge, and the Reaper is the middleman.

"Death," The Reaper addresses me politely. When I flick my gaze to the beautiful human girl, I realize we made the right decision with her. Fate already knows, of course. She knows all and orchestrates it beautifully.

"Reaper, why don't you visit your beloved Gods anymore?" I proclaim.

"Many apologies, my Lord." He bows his head. "I have been busy Reaping… and visiting her."

I wave him off. I know that.

Before I could speak again, my wife saunters into the room dressed in gorgeous traditional white and baby blue robes that almost seem to float with her, making her look fantastic. She has always loved a good entrance. Instead of walking to her throne beside mine, she goes to The Reaper and the human girl. "Reaper, hello."

"Fate, lovely as always," he responds and bows his head. The girl nervously tucks herself further behind him. She sends The Reaper a soft smile. She has always had a soft spot in her heart for him. As do I. Fate and I have each other, but The Reaper has been alone for centuries, which is why the girl stands before us now.

"Hello, child." Fate's voice is smooth and soothing. "Do not be afraid."

She grabs the girl under her chin and moves her head left and right to inspect her. The girl lets her, inspecting her with her own big doe eyes, but then asks, "Are you a God?"

"I am, my sweet, as is my husband, Death. The Reaper, although, is not." She pauses, using her abilities to sense the girl's emotions. "That relieves you?"

"Yes," the girl answers. "He would intimidate me if he were… my Lady."

"Don't worry, Darling. I am more like an entity." The Reaper says, reassuring her and looking down at her. Then he reluctantly says, "Are you ready to move on?" The girl hesitates and then says, "I don't want to leave you."

Fate smiles and then glides up the stairs to her throne and greets me, "My love."

"Hello, beautiful," I respond. My wife is smug because her plan has worked. She saw the potential for this human girl and has orchestrated a match. The rest worked out for itself. Fate can only do so much; she can only set up the dominos, but she can't make them fall. "I have come to a decision…"

The Reaper sits atop a ledge on the Empire State Building all alone. The city is so beautiful at this time of day, just before the sun sets, where the sky is a perfect shade of soft, golden light. One foot is swinging over the side, and the other is tucked to his chest.

Memory floats up to The Reaper from behind, startling him by saying, "Hello, my handsome Reaper."

"Hello, Darling." A huge smile takes over his face as he looks at Memory, his beautiful companion. She circles him as a cat would and then sits next to him on the ledge. She is even more beautiful now than she was as a human – because now she is a graceful, ethereal creature. Her skin is almost translucent white, and her hair the same shade. All while maintaining her doe eyes, small lips, and a button nose from when she was human. The most notable change is that her legs have disappeared, and in their place, multi-colored smoke that trails behind her. "What're you doing up here?" she asks.

"Watching the sunset," he responds, "Are you famous yet?"

"My bridge painting just sold for one point three million dollars." Memory says excitedly. "And all the money is going to my dad. So not only am I famous, but I'm happy, and my dad is taken care of."

"I am so glad for you."

He leans over and presses their foreheads together but doesn't initiate a kiss. She closes the distance and presses a brief kiss to his lips, then pulls away and puts her head on his shoulder with a content smile. Enjoying his company and the sunset alike.

They both get the feeling of a death in this very city. Getting there in a second, a young woman is sitting dead in her car after a pretty traumatizing car wreck. They are met with a scared young woman standing next to her body but facing away from it.

"Hello, Alice." the Reaper says, veiling her emotions with calm.

"Hello," the woman says, confused, a tremble in her voice. "Who are you?" "I am The Reaper of Souls. This is my companion Memory," The Reaper answers, gesturing to Memory.

"Hello, Alice," Memory says, approaching the woman.

"I'm dead? Are you taking me to the afterlife?"

"You are… but we will only leave when you are ready." The Reaper answers. Alice takes a moment to decide, glancing at her body briefly, but her eyes don't linger. Her terrifying, bloodied body is too foul a sight to gaze at for long. The Reaper can tell she's ready to leave this world behind. "I am ready. I want to see my family."

"We will take you to them, but first, can we show you something?" Memory asks gently. This is a new method of reaping Memory has decided upon, asking instead of just immediately pushing them into their past.

"Yes?" Alice answers. The Reaper snaps his fingers, and they are in a hospital. Alice being born with such vividness that The Reaper can even see a small blemish on her mom's chin and the sweat tracing down her eyebrows.

This is where Memory shines, why she was reborn. The Reaper unawarely didn't make the walk down memory lane very enjoyable to the souls, just flashed from scene to scene, not letting them reminisce or enjoy their life. Memory paints elegant pictures and beautiful scenery. She stops at memories the soul likes the most, breeze by the upsetting ones. Every memory is important and deserves their time in the wake after your death.

In Alice's case, they walk through beautiful hikes that she has enjoyed over the years. The forest becomes real. The humidity in the air sticks to their skin, and birds chirp in the trees.

When she got her first job in a small cubical, they get the feeling of being compressed in an office that was actually two square feet wide. Then quitting that job to scribble poems under a large oak tree while basking under the sun's warm rays, they can smell the freshly cut grass and sunscreen breezing through the air. Then when she conquered Everest not once, but twice. The wind is chilly and the most beautiful sight – besides watching her son being born – she had ever seen lay out in front of her exactly as she saw it. Finally, when she met her wife and when they had their baby boy. Alice could even smell her son's head, just like the first time she held him. By the end of it, Alice is balling her eyes out.

The Reaper asks. "Do you want to see your family now?"

Alice can only manage a nod, So The Reaper snaps his fingers again, and they are all standing at Death's door. Every single one of her family members are standing outside alongside her wife and her young son. She was completely alone in her life… no family, no love – her entire family was here in the afterlife.

Alice trips over herself to run and embrace her family.

"Oh, Hija!" her mother coos.

Alice can't stop from crying, tears continually pouring down her face. "Mama." Her wife and son are crying too. "Baby, I missed you so, so much. I love you so much." "I love you too. I love you so so much." Her wife responds.

"Rest in peace." Memory and The Reaper say at the same time and vanish together. Off to reap and guide and soothe and love.

Off together, no longer alone in this no longer bleak world.

The Wedding

Leilani Johnson

Lilah Castorini couldn't remember the last time she put on a dress. The one she wore now had spaghetti straps and a cinched-in waist, the kind that made her feel as though all of her stomach rolls were being folded like a dirty heap of laundry. Her parents had dragged her to one of her cousin's weddings on a day off from school. Quite frankly, she couldn't remember exactly which cousin; all she knew was that she had heard the name "Julie" when her mother read the invitation aloud at the kitchen table earlier that week.

She and her family showed up late to the reception. They were coming from out of town, unfamiliar with the sprawling streets of downtown Detroit. When they finally arrived at the venue— the bride and groom had chosen a towering rooftop that overlooked the city —her mother snaked her hand around Lilah's waist in an ironclad snare.

"I'm cold," Lilah deadpanned.

Her mother just smiled through clenched teeth.

Lilah's older brother flounced away to find the nearest tray of food. Her dad asked her mother if she wanted to find Ronny, her third-cousin-twice-removed ("He just got a new job working in commerce!"), and Lilah used that as an opening to slip away. She slunk to the edge of the rooftop, away from the crowd, and picked at the split ends of her cuticles. Down on the street below, she could just barely make out the shapes of three jazz musicians piping blues through their saxophones. The sharp trill of each note was like the calling of a bird.

Above her, the sky was a murky shade of indigo, the kind that forms when a toddler mixes too many watercolors at once. But stretched across the clouds, as if stolen from a savannah, was a single slash of crimson.

It looks bloody, Lilah thought, like a Scab.

She turned over her shoulder and saw her parents mingling with guests in an assembly line fashion. Every time that her dad shifted his weight closer to her mother, she would bristle, wait a few seconds, then step a millimeter away from him, all while keeping a smile on her face that would make the judge of a beauty pageant proud.

At least I'm not a bride, Lilah told herself.

She searched the party for someone she could fixate on. At last, her eyes locked on the bartender, a lanky young man with gaunt fingers that curled around each wine glass as he handed them to sluggish guests. His eyes met hers as she emerged like a phantom in front of him. "Hello," she said.

"Hello," he said and regarded her dubiously, partially amused. "Can I get you something?" He motioned to an array of bottles stacked in front of him, all of which glimmered translucently like orbed eyes severed from their sockets.

She shook her head and stated simply, "I don't drink."

He nodded as if he heard this all the time working as a bartender. "Well then, how do you know the groom?" Then he added, "Or the bride?"

And Lilah found herself saying before she could stop herself, "I don't."

There was a long silence, punctuated by a bulbous man in a too-small suit who demanded that the bartender "fetch a bloody mary" for some leggy blonde girl at his side. With a robotic detachment, the bartender attacked the faucets and levers in front of him, the bits and nobs that sputtered this way and that, until he set a blood-red drink on the counter with unproud finality. The man whisked his date away without another word, and it wasn't until they left that Lilah noticed a bulged vein road-mapping across the bartender's temple. He smelled sickeningly sweet, like wilted flowers on an un-sunned porch.

Without meeting her eyes, he murmured, "I like this song." He hesitated. "Do you want to dance?" And when she stared back at him blankly, he begged breathlessly into her ear— "Do you want to dance?"

Before she could respond, a hand snaked around her shoulder, and with an instinctive lurch, she realized it was her mother.

She leaned into Lilah's ear and cooed, "You simply must see Hank and Nicole's baby. You simply must."

And before she could protest, Lilah was whisked away, dragged through swarms of people who didn't bother stepping aside when she said, "Excuse me."

Sitting at a table was Nicole, a cousin that Lilah actually recognized. In fact, she quite liked Nicole. She and her husband, Hank, had let Lilah retreat to their basement to draw pictures in her notebook when they hosted a family dinner party two years prior. Nicole was petite and soft-spoken, the kind of person Lilah would've liked to have as a school teacher. "Lilah!" Nicole smiled warmly. "My, how you've grown!"

Lilah mustered a smile in return. She usually hated when adults started conversations that way, but with Nicole, it didn't feel so artificial.

"Have you held Abigail?" Lilah's mother interjected.

Lilah froze. "Uh…"

Nicole's eyes widened. "Oh, you have to hold her! You just have to!"

And before Lilah could admit that she had never really been the best with children or that she wasn't even sure she liked children after she babysat for a stubby-legged rugrat named

Cody, this past summer, who chucked mud grenades at the back of her head whenever she took him outside to play, her mother placed both hands on her back and thrusted her forward against her will.

A nearby friend carefully handed Nicole a cocoon of blankets. Each fold of the fabric was meticulously embroidered with tiny pink strawberries. "Hello, darling," Nicole sing-songed, and the cocoon began to squirm. Then— the doe-like whimper of an infant bubbled through the air. Lilah's mother clapped her hand over her heart and swooned. Lilah, on the other hand, felt her stomach begin to churn.

Nicole caressed the child with a brush of her fingertips. Her words came out in a hushed whisper: "This is Abigail."

She looked at Lilah expectantly. At first, Lilah didn't move. Then her mother prodded her forward with a dangerous glimmer of her eyes.

Nicole handed her the baby slowly, making sure to support her head. Lilah swallowed hard and instinctively created a basin with her arms for the child to sink into. Nicole sat back in her chair and beamed. "See? You got it." She glanced at Lilah's mother, who smiled back proudly. Lilah fought the urge to roll her eyes.

She glanced down gingerly as if bracing herself for the letter "F" at the top of a math test. Then her eyes locked on the child's immediately— Abigail's eyes. They were wide and inquisitive, and suddenly Lilah couldn't look away. She felt something bloom in her chest. "How precious," Nicole whispered.

She repositioned Abigail on her lap, with one arm securely wrapped around her belly. The baby was plush like a wad of pastry dough, and suddenly Lilah felt the overwhelming urge to knead her with her knuckles until flour purged from her pores. Nicole smiled at Lilah, who smiled back without meeting her gaze. Abigail reached up and grappled for her hair with slippery fingers as if trying to climb a bundle of vines. A giggle escaped her lips. It sounded like springtime.

Hank appeared at Nicole's side. "Honey," he cooed softly. "Julie needs your help mending her dress."

A stillness crept into the air. Nicole didn't move. Her eyes flitted to Lilah, then down to Abigail. Lilah felt the pads of her fingers press deeper into the baby's dimpled arms. "I'll be here with her," Lilah's mother cut in. She flashed Nicole a reassuring smile. Nicole smiled back, but her eyes bristled. Before Lilah could say anything, Hank huffed in exasperation. "Honestly, darling. We can't wait all day." He turned over his shoulder and met Lilah's eyes sheepishly as if apologizing for his wife's concern.

Nicole hesitated. Then finally, with the helpless glance of a deer, she let Hank steer her away.

Abigail flashed Lilah a gummy grin. She brushed her thumb across the bottom of the baby's chin and smiled at the warmth of her body.

"Okay, darling." Her mother's voice was laced with ice. "Let me hold her." All at once, Lilah's spine turned rigid. Abigail slipped slightly on her knee. The infant pressed her hands into Lilah's chest as if forcing open a door.

"What, baby?" she whispered. "What is it?"

"Darling," her mother repeated. "Give her here."

She pretended not to notice. Abigail pressed her hands to Lilah's chest again, then stretched upward so high that she fumbled in her grasp.

"The sky?" Lilah whispered in her ear. "You want the sky?"

"Darling," Mother hissed, and this time she tried to grab the baby.

Lilah rose to her feet, holding Abigail securely in her arms. Mother's eyes darted left and right. Abigail whimpered, curling closer to Lilah's body. She nuzzled her chin into the baby's bed of hair.

Then she began to walk.

"Lilah," her mother called after her. "Lilah." But she was moving too fast, oozing like ink through the throngs of wedding guests. Lilah knew Mother wouldn't run after her. She wouldn't want to cause a scene in front of the other guests. No, absolutely not.

"Don't worry," she assured the child. "I've got you." They drifted through the dance floor, past sweat-drenched men in tuxedos and women in too-tight bustiers, all of whom were jumping up and down without rhythm like an ocean of spilled marbles.

"Lilah!" a voice called. Her dad floated towards his daughter, a skewered cocktail shrimp in his right hand. "Where's the restroom?" When she didn't answer, his eyes locked on the baby swaddled in her arms, like he just noticed that she was there.

Lilah tightened her grip on Abigail as if shielding a diorama that she had made for a middle school science fair. With two more quick strides, she reached the row of dining tables that crowned the rooftop. Each of them was small, circular, and draped with creamy white cloth that glimmered like cake fondant.

"See?" she whispered to the child. "Do you see it?" She pointed to the Scab. It was still there, emblazoned across the clouds. "Do you need me to get closer?"

A couple looked up at her from their table. She ignored them and stepped towards the edge of the roof.

"See it?"

She tilted the baby's head softly with her palm until her eyes finally locked on the expanse of crimson. Abigail let out a sigh of wonderment through her dribbly lips. It was the same sigh that Lilah had made when she was an infant, on the one year that her mom agreed to bake her a homemade chocolate cake for her birthday, and she reached her hand down from the kitchen countertop so that Lilah could suck a dollop of icing off her thumb. By this time, a crowd had begun to form.

Except, Lilah wasn't aware of this until she felt the absence of music in the air. She turned over her shoulder and saw a flock of wedding guests slowly inching towards her, the same way a collapsed tidal wave reaches for a child's toes on the shore of a beach.

At the helm of the ship was her mother.

"W-what are you doing?" she breathed.

Lilah was alarmed at her tone. Every guest seemed dumbstruck. Her mother's eyes were filled with a terror that she didn't recognize. Her dad, obviously not too preoccupied with finding the bathroom after all, was standing at her mother's side. Even her brother was there, with half of his suit buttoned disproportionately so that one side of his collar was raised higher than the other. Lilah might have laughed if she hadn't been so confused.

"Please," her mother stammered. "Take her down."

Lilah didn't understand. Abigail had wanted to see the sky. So she showed her. "Where is she?" a voice cried. "Where is she?"

The crowd rippled, and all of a sudden, Nicole was at the front. Her hand clapped over her mouth as soon as she saw her daughter.

"Please." Her face was drained of all color. "Please, give her to me."

Lilah glanced at Abigail. Her eyes, pure and pearlescent, were still on the Scab. A warmth flooded through Lilah's chest like she had never known.

"She wants to get closer," Lilah replied. "You wouldn't understand."

Nicole's mouth crumpled. She implored,

"That's my daughter."

Lilah's mouth pressed into a thin line. She stared at Nicole. Tears—big, gloppy, and monstrous—were streaming down her face. The other wedding guests stood in a lily pond of dread, except for a single person in the very back, who seemed rather awestruck by the scene in front of him. It was the bartender.

Then Lilah looked at her mother, who stood like a stranger.

She let go of Abigail. The baby fumbled for a moment, then disappeared off the edge of the roof.

There was a bloodcurdling scream. Someone rushed forward and knocked Lilah to the ground.

As her head hit the pavement, she could still hear the crooning of saxophones from down on the street below.

The Sirens Are Coming
-Winner-

Chloe Ross

The Gilded Age of Piracy, as its name suggests, designates the period of time when the highest number of pirates in history openly sailed the seas… At this time, like Imperial vessels of today, many of the ships employed Vaytus and Apaqi to help guide ships and increase a vessel's speed (if the reader is not familiar with the wind and water abilities of Vaytus and Apaqi, respectively, then I advise them to read my other work, *An Idiot's Guide to Vedruya and it's Users*, in which I cover in-depth the history of all four vedruya-users). Because of this, a life of piracy was especially common for these ability-users.

- an excerpt from the prologue of *A General History of Pirates* by Wilbur Oswood

One of the pirate's most feared opponents was not the Empire, which was still in its formative years, but instead was the siren. Sirens have the lower body of a shark, their upper bodies are similar to that of a woman's except for the fact that it is as dark as their tails and often patched with scales, and their hair acts as a sensory organ. They are born from violent deaths, coming into being when a girl is forcefully drowned, murdered at sea, commits suicide by jumping into the sea, or is cruelly killed and then has their body dumped into the ocean (if the reader wishes to know more about sirens, I would direct them to my other work, *Twins of Good and Evil: A Guide to Mermaids and Sirens*).

- an excerpt from chapter seven of *A General History of Pirates* by Wilbur Oswood

All Kendra wanted was a glass of her finest red wine. The kind that she had to balance between her fingers, careful not to spill a drop as she rocked with the movement of the sea. Instead, she was jammed into a rickety lifeboat, trapped in a dress two sizes too small. Her thin beige fingers pleated and un-pleated the red satin skirts where they draped around her, taking up almost all the room in the rickety vessel. Although, it wasn't even fair to call these tacked-together pieces of rotten wood, the only thing between her and the unforgiving sea, a vessel. Kendra shuddered at the thought. Without thinking, her fingers strayed back to her sleeve cuffs, tugging them down further over her wrists, making sure they were covering her forearms. She didn't realize that she'd done this fourteen times already.

Throughout her life, she'd had a difficult relationship with waiting. Oftentimes she scorned it, shoving it aside and taking action when it needed to be taken. She'd learned too harshly, and too late the consequences that would come when waiting was scorned. However, in times like this, she needed to befriend waiting, coax it out from its hiding spot, and learn to live with it.

The sun was just starting to bleed into the water when Kendra finally saw the outline of a ship. But still, she waited. She couldn't afford to make any mistakes. Especially not tonight. It was only when the ship was close enough that she could read in the dying light the name scrawled on its side—Najaizder; Raider—that she moved, standing up abruptly and ignoring the violent rocking of the lifeboat beneath her.

"Help me! Over here—please help me!" she cried, desperation bleeding into her voice, her arms frantically waving above her head.

"And why would I do that, darling?" a voice responded. Kendra squinted a bit as she looked out, and she could just make out the man's profile against the setting sun, his golden hair illuminated by the light and his bored eyes glinting. He was looking at Kendra like she was an annoying barnacle he'd happened to find on the sole of his boot.

Kendra crossed her arms and tilted her chin up to the man.

"Why wouldn't you help a poor soul stranded in the middle of the ocean?"

The man barked out a laugh, throwing his head back. "Oh, a feisty one, aren't you? Let's see if that fire stays when the sirens come out at night and make you their meal." Kendra let her eyes widen as if shocked by his words. "I know what you are," she said, and her voice shook with fear. "A bloody pirate! Forget it. I'd rather you leave me here to die." She promptly sat back down, turning her back to the ship.

"Come now, don't be like that, darling," the man said with a warm chuckle. "I could never leave a pretty thing like you to be lost to the sirens."

I already am, Kendra thought.

"And besides," the man continued, "pirates aren't all bad. If you have something to trade, I'll let you aboard."

Kendra glanced at the man over her shoulder. She wavered for a second, weighing her choices. Then she stood as she lifted a golden medallion from around her neck. "Would this do?" she asked, holding it up and letting the dying light catch its golden edges.

"That little thing?" the man laughed. "I'm not that easy, darling."

"That's too bad," Kendra tutted, lowering her head. She started playing with the medallion, twirling it around her fist, catching it, twirling it the other way, catching it, and repeating. "Then you wouldn't mind if I dropped it, would you?" Kendra asked airily. "It's an old family heirloom. Royal blood's said to have worn it ages ago, but apparently, you don't care for that. Maybe the sirens would take up my deal if I just," she looked right at the man above her, "let it go." She opened her hand and let it fall through her fingers—

"Wait!" the man said, his voice tight with panic and greed. Kendra caught the chain at the very last second. "Royal blood, you say?"

"Mhm," Kendra hummed in acknowledgment.

The man chuckled. "You play a cruel game, darling."

And you don't even know the half of it.

"I do have one condition, though," Kendra called up to the man.

"Of course you do." Kendra could almost hear him rolling his eyes. "What is it?" "You must swear on vedruya to grant me shelter and safe passage and that no harm shall come to me. Deal?"

"I swear it, darling." The sun was almost gone, but Kendra didn't have to see his smirk to hear it in his voice. She knew what he was thinking: stupid girl, to think a pirate would keep his word. It's what she would think in his shoes.

"On vedruya," she insisted.

"On vedruya."

"Very well."

"Marvelous!" the man said sharply, clapping his hands together. "Tarle," he called over his shoulder, "help this poor lass get up here, won't you?"

"Right away, captain," a voice responded.

Kendra heard the unfurling of a rope ladder and watched as a shadow detached itself from the ship and landed in the lifeboat beside her, causing it to rock violently. Tarle pulled on the rope to draw them even with the side of Najaizder, then unceremoniously hauled her over his shoulder like a sack of potatoes and started climbing. Kendra gritted her teeth and forced her hands to still. But by all the Sveti, she wanted nothing more than to gauge out this man's eye for his audacity.

Kendra landed on the deck a bit awkwardly, and her delicate shoes twisted as she stumbled, but the man—captain—was there, gripping her elbow lightly to stabilize her. Then he shamelessly held out his hand. Kendra drew herself to her full height and looked the captain dead in the eyes as she dropped the medallion into his waiting palm, the chain clinking softly as it fell. As he held the medallion up to a lantern, Kendra fell back into the habits she'd had to drill into her very bones. Don't avert your eyes, don't let them know. Reach out. How many people are there? What are the exits? Think of everything like a puzzle: learn it and crack it. Three men on watch, two of whom had been standing near the bow but were coming towards her, the other, Tarle, who was standing just a few steps away. There were two who she didn't even need to turn to—she saw them stop shuffling cards the moment she arrived on deck and could feel their eyes burning suspicious holes into the back of her skull. The captain, who was standing before her. Probably four belowdecks, if there were three men per watch group and the cook. Eleven men, round up to fifteen to account for assumption errors.

Kendra refocused her attention on the captain. He was studying the medallion, a slight furrow between his brows. If anyone saw the medallion up close, they would immediately be able to tell that it was an obvious ploy. From afar, its golden sheen caught the light and gleamed like true gold, but up close, you could see how the paint was peeling off the cheap metal, the chain rusted to the point that any sharp movement would break it. Finally, the captain looked back at Kendra. For a while, they just stared at each other. Kendra realized that the captain was younger than she'd originally thought, probably only in his mid-twenties, not much older or younger than she was, at her twenty-four years of age. His sandy hair was tousled like he'd formed a habit of running his hands through it, and no one had ever told him to stop. Eventually, he threw his head back and let out a raucous laugh.

"Oh, I like this one. Can we keep her?" he asked no one in particular, his voice heavy with mirth.

Kendra simply raised a single disdainful eyebrow. When he received no other response, the captain stepped close to her, lifting her chin with a single finger. Kendra wanted to break it. "Now, I'm just curious about one thing: what made you think you could trick me, Alastair Beckett, the most feared pirate on the seas—" Kendra wrinkled her nose a bit at that "—with a rusting piece of junk? Or are you just as stupid as you are pretty?" Kendra resisted rolling her eyes. If she really tried, she could trick him blindfolded and with both hands tied behind her back. But she would let him think he'd figured her out, seen through her lies. Even if he only knew he was tricked because she wanted him to. "I knew I couldn't trick you forever," was all Kendra said, "but at least it worked long enough for me to get you to swear on vedruya."

Alastair stepped back, letting go of her chin. He hummed and tilted his head, trying to get a read on her. But eventually, all he said was, "That I did. And I always keep my word." His voice formed those last words, dripping with falsity. The crew members on deck quickly stifled their chuckles.

When Kendra didn't say anything else, Alastair nodded his head and gestured towards the stern. "Go down that hatch, and there's an empty room on the starboard side you can use. That'll be where you'll stay until we reach land."

But Kendra didn't move. Instead, she tilted her head as if she were still confused and lost. "What's on the port?"

Alastair had started to walk away but turned back to her at that, obviously not expecting the question. "That's where the crew sleeps."

"And if I keep going? What's at the end of the passageway?"

Alastair gave her a quick once over and winked. "That's where I sleep, darling." Kendra rolled her eyes and sharply turned on her heel, making her way toward the stern hatch. As she descended the ladder, she passed two men coming the opposite direction and let them pass, ignoring their curious and wandering gazes. Kendra waited until she heard their footsteps above her, then quickly poked her head through the port side door. Her brief count came up with ten hammocks and the appropriate amount of luggage to match. Eleven men. Kendra ducked out of the doorway and was grinning as she entered her own room. The room Kendra was to use was much smaller. She had to duck her head to avoid the brass pipes overhead and had to watch her step around crates overflowing with tools, both for ship maintenance and navigation. In the corner of the room, she found a small cot, obviously discarded, the stuffing coming out and dark spots of something Kendra didn't want to look too closely at. At least she would never be sleeping here. Kendra gave the cot a wide berth and sat instead on an overturned crate, cushioning her skirts beneath her to make her seat more comfortable.

Phase one of her plan was a success. Now all she could do was wait.

If the pirates didn't kill Kendra, the boredom would.

She stayed begrudgingly with waiting, tolerating its presence as she sat like a statue in the dark, not moving a muscle, listening to the sounds of the waking all around her. Sounds that were slowly fading away into snores and restful murmuring as the night grew later. It was when Kendra heard only three pairs of footsteps above her head that she got to work.

The first thing Kendra did was lift the skirts of her dress and pick at the knot of the stocking she'd fashioned into a garter, releasing the knife that had been tied to her thigh and placing it on the crate. Even sheathed, she could sense the ancient vedruya of the weapon, the carvings etched on its blade reacting to the matching scars on her forearms as if they knew what was coming. It made the old wounds ache again. But Kendra kept going, drawing the following from the many pockets she'd sewn into the dress: her normal clothes, a scarf and scrap of twine, two reinforced leather bases and buckles, and three small vials with what appeared to be black smoke inside. Then Kendra took the knife, unsheathed it (she ignored the way it whispered to her, like a lover), and cut the strings on the back of the dress. She shucked the thing off and threw it onto the cot in the corner. They could both rot in hell. Even after quickly changing into her clothes— high-waisted black pants with golden buttons and a long sleeve off-white blouse—she still felt naked. She rubbed the exposed skin on her forearms that her leather vambraces usually covered. But she shook the feeling off and quickly tied her hair out of her face with the twine, then sat back on the crate and, with the leather and buckles, covered the high heel of her shoe with a solid-based platform. She picked the vials up from where they rested beside her and slid them into the holder on her waist, excessively careful not to crack their thin glass. Kendra hesitated before grabbing her knife but nestled it into the straps on her right thigh anyways. It felt wrong having it out in the open, but she needed easy access to it tonight. It was the only weapon she'd brought on board. Her hips felt lighter, almost empty, without the familiar weight of her sword on her left and pistol on her right, but she couldn't risk bringing them. Not tonight. For this job, all she had was her knife, her power, and her wits.

The scarf was the last thing Kendra took with her. Instead of tying it around her head, she used it to cover her nose and mouth. As she opened the door to the room she was in, an old sea shanty came into her head.

Music, like vedruya, holds memories. A simple tune can take you into a different place, into a different time. And so, for just a moment, Kendra was fourteen again: an icy island faded into the sea behind her, her hand held tightly and blood drying beneath her nails, and the voice of her loved one singing to her. But memories are just memories. Kendra was not fourteen anymore, and she could no longer hold the hand of her loved one.

Kendra started singing under her breath as she grabbed one of the vials.

How do you know when the sirens are coming?

(Coming, they're coming for you.)

The door to the room across the hall opened only a sliver before Kendra threw the vial inside. She heard it smash and shut the door firmly behind her. She continued up the ladder but paused before her head would be visible from the deck. Kendra reached out. Vedruya was there, waiting for her, its dark energy welcoming her back. It had been a long time since she'd openly used her power, and it was as if the thing could sense it. Kendra had nudged it a bit before when she'd sensed how many men were on the ship and later when she'd unsheathed her knife. But now that she was openly calling upon it, it was basking in the attention, stroking her cheek and playing with her hair like a long-parted lover. Kendra let the energy surround her like a dark mantle. She didn't need it to be honed into a knife's blade now. Not yet, at least.

If the sea turns dark and thick as blood.

(The sea, it turns to blood.)

Kendra took a deep breath, rolled her shoulders, and walked confidently above deck. As she stepped out, she let one of the vials roll in front of her then crushed it with her boot. The crew members on watch glanced over at the sound of her footsteps. One was the man, Tarle, that had brought her aboard, and the other two were a lanky boy with red hair and an older man.

"Is it time for the next watch already?" the lanky boy asked, holding his lantern higher. "No, not yet. I think it's the girl we picked up earlier," Tarle replied, picking out her silhouette in the moonlight.

"Oh, you are bright," Kendra crooned, but her grin had fangs.

"Hey, what are you doing?" Tarle said, drawing a short sword as she drew closer, and the light fell across her face. "You shouldn't be out here."

Kendra walked up to him, and her hand hovered just above his face, close enough to cup his cheek. "Shouldn't I?" she drawled, looking deep into the man's eyes. "How do you know what I should be doing? In fact, how do you know what I, what anyone, is doing at all? Isn't this all just a bad dream?"

And Kendra reached. She didn't stay long in Tarle's head. Her power already knew what to do (it had practiced so much on her, after all). At first, it almost seemed as if the ship was flooding. Around Tarle, dark shadowy water slowly rose, leaving him trapped and starting to lose his access to air.

Kendra was quickly brought out of her ponderings by a wave of heat that just missed her right side. She hissed and whirled around, drawing her knife while she did. The lanky boy with red hair was holding a torch in his hand. No, not a torch. Just the flame. And Kendra could see soft swirls and harsh angles on the insides of his forearms, lit from within with a soft red glow. He was Agimma. This was going to be a fun fight.

The two circled each other, one illuminated by flickering light, the other wreathed in black shadows. As Kendra studied his face, she saw that it held no fear in it. The boy struck first.

Instead of moving against the fire, like how most pirates Kendra had fought would avoid a strike, Kendra moved with it, dancing around the flame and using its light to blind her opponent. He brought his hand up to shield his eyes, and Kendra dodged into his blind spot, slashing at his palm with her knife. Then, just as quickly, she danced out of his range, avoiding the wall of fire he'd raised in front of him in response to her strike.

As soon as the fire went down, her opponent having realized that Kendra wasn't there anymore, she moved towards him. When he raised his hand to send the fire towards her, she quickened her pace and whirled behind him, slashing at his side.

The boy glared at her but didn't make a move back. Instead, he started walking, and they circled each other once more. Obviously, he hadn't thought her to be such a strong opponent. He needed to strategize.

When the boy moved again, it was a sloppy strike, slowed by the drugged smoke in the vial, the fire going toward Kendra's head. She ducked easily, then swerved right to avoid another ball of flame. Each attack was starting to get slower and messier. Now she could see panic in his eyes.

Kendra started running towards the boy, and he backed away quickly, randomly throwing fire around. Kendra swerved each one easily, and her power pooled in her palms as she reached him. Now that he was scared, she could use vedruya against him. She dropped into a slide at the last minute, knocking the boy off his feet, then quickly was back up on her knees above him, covering his mouth and nose with her hands, stealing the breath from his lungs. Ten.

Kendra stood up. The older man had already succumbed to the smoke.

Nine.

Kendra left the bodies where they lay and walked over to Tarle. The smoky water had almost covered his head now. She nudged it down a bit until he was able to take a shaking breath again. His cheeks were stained with tears.

"I'm scared," Tarle cried, and his voice was like that of a child.

"I know," Kendra replied.

"Please, make it stop. Make it all stop," he begged, fresh tears rolling down his cheeks. Kendra called her shadows back, drawing the drugged smoke into them. They choked Tarle, and as Kendra walked away, she heard his body fall to the deck.

Eight.

Kendra stepped over the bodies and walked down the ladder.

If they're maidens or virgins or murdered or drowned.

(Or drowned, or drowned below.)

Kendra heard screams and wails dying off as she entered the crew's barracks and noticed that most had already fallen.

Seven.

Six.

Five.

Four.

She knew she only had to wait for the others to fall, so she simply leaned against the doorway, needing to see the work done, willing to welcome waiting again.

When their skin is scales and dark as stone.

(Their scales, they're dark as stone.)

This time, she didn't need to sit and feed, waiting for long.

Three.

Two.

One.

The room grew quiet. All of them had fallen still, and slowly her shadows dissipated, slinking back to her like a child seeking praise. Kendra hummed her tune.

When they cut through water with shattering song.

(Their song, their song will kill.)

Kendra stepped back out into the passageway, but before she could make her way to the captain's room, she felt a sharp pain in her side. She quickly whirled around and saw Alastair behind her, holding a sword.

"That was only a warning, darling," he drawled, his voice full of hollow overconfidence.

"You're in my way," Kendra growled. "Move."

"As much as I would like to, I'm afraid I can't do that."

Kendra didn't wait for him to finish. Halfway through his sentence, she'd lunged at him, catching him off guard and smashing her last vial in his face. She could hear him coughing as she bounded up the stairs. Her scarf helped keep the drug out, but he didn't want to take any chances. When she was above deck, she whirled around and saw Alastair coming after her, his eyes watering, coughs still escaping from his throat.

Kendra rolled her eyes. "You're persistent; I'll give you that."

"Why shouldn't I be? You killed my crew." Even now, he kept his voice level, like he was commenting on the weather.

"You don't seem too upset," Kendra retorted.

"You don't seem too guilty," he shot back. "Look at you," he drawled, "so smug and satisfied with your bloody work, thinking that you've won. But this means nothing to me. I will kill you and throw your body into the seas to be food to the sirens. Then, after I spend a bit of time in the arms of my lovely Jo, I'll just hire a new crew. You will lose everything while all I waste is time."

Kendra knew he was monologuing, stalling for time. But at the mention of that name, she could not stop the memories. They came at her in waves, short crimson hair tickling her face, a lingering kiss on her cheek, a mischievous laugh ringing in her ear. They brought back the phantom sensation of a sorrow so deep it tore her throat when she screamed and carved her empty when she cried. The edges of her vision went red, and her knuckles whitened as her hands balled into fists.

"Jo?" she spat the word at him, hoping it would cut him. But her words had acted against her, betraying her true feelings.

Alastair's grin turned victorious at the slip. "Is that a bit of humanity I see, darling? Sympathy for poor Josie, the tavern lass on shore that takes my money to lie on her back with her legs spread? You have no compassion for your fellow pirates, but your heart bleeds for a common whore?"

Not your Jo. Kendra thought, and the memories receded for now. Not your Josanna. Kendra had to act now. She couldn't let him regain the upper hand. Even though Alastair seemed calm,

Kendra had learned to read fear better than anyone. She formed vedruya into a sword to match his and pointed it directly at his chest. His eyes widened, flashing from the sword to her forearms back to her face, and he gripped his own blade tighter.

"We can do this two ways," Kendra said. "I can kill you quickly, or I can make it very, very painful. You saw what I did to the rest of your crew; you saw the agony on their faces. It's your choice."

"Unfortunately, both options result in me ending up dead, so I'd like to avoid those." "Too bad," Kendra scoffed. "Now choose." Her shadows rose around Alastair, restricting his movements and preventing him from lifting his sword. He looked at Kendra as she walked towards him, his fear finally bleeding into his eyes.

"What are you?"

Kendra gave a wicked grin. It was the kind of smile that only comes from the pages of fairy tales, the kind of smile that belongs to the monsters that are distinctly not human. She whispered in Alastair's ear.

"Your worst nightmare."

Kendra slit his throat and stepped over the body. She released her shadows and felt vedruya retreat through her veins. She unwound the scarf from around her face and tilted her head back to the moonlight, welcoming the fresh sea air in her lungs.

How do you know when the sirens are coming?

(Coming, they're coming for you.)

You won't see them coming 'till you're dead on the deck.

'Till your blood spills like ink in the sea.

An Indian Summer

Pravallika Kullampalle

He carefully surveyed my face before taking hold of my cheek, squeezing it tight enough to turn my cinnamon complexion rosy.

"Ow!" I cried out as I rubbed my cheek. Would I ever grow out of this greeting? I wondered as I looked up at a man who beamed down at me.

"Look at how much you have grown, Anni! You look just like Nana. You know, they say it is good fortune when a daughter looks like her father." he said as he handed me a bouquet of roses that had given into the heat of the monsoon season. "Now, tell me, how was your journey? I was worried when you told me you were flying alone." my Babai said, taking the handle of the cart of suitcases in front of me.

"The journey was good, Babai. My ears didn't pop when we were landing, thank God. See, I told you that you were worried for nothing." I responded in Telugu, hoping my false confidence would mask the panic attack I had moments earlier.

My thoughts had run to worst-case scenarios as I struggled to balance a backpack, a camera slung over my shoulder, and a cart of suitcases. The airport terminal was filled with cab drivers holding signs reading the names of people I didn't know and anxious family members holding welcome home signs. As my eyes drifted from eager faces to impatient ones, a bubble of panic started to rise within me. It wasn't until I set my eyes on a dark, broad-shouldered man in a worn checkered flannel who was struggling to capture my attention as he waved his hands high above his head did I stop and take a deep breath. The bubble burst inside me as I pushed my cart in my Uncle's direction.

"Welcome to India!" he had exclaimed, just like the last time I had seen him and the time before.

Our conversation continued as my Babai pushed the cart up through the airport's parking lot. A tall, balding man dressed similarly to my Babai waved his hand as we approached him. "The luggage, I will put, you sit in car. You have good journey?" the driver said in broken English as he pointed toward the car. I stifled a giggle before responding.

"Driver Uncle, Nenu Telugu Matladuthaanu, Journey baaga ayindi," I speak Telugu. Yes, the journey went well. After close to twenty-four hours of traveling, it felt good to breathe in the outdoor air around me. The humid air smelled of a medley of the airport's outdoor food court and a sleeping city. I settled into the window seat of the car as the driver and my Babai worked to tie the suitcases to the top of the car. I rolled down the windows and closed my eyes. My favorite part of the journey still lay ahead of me: A four-hour drive from the Bangalore Airport to the small town of Pantapalli. After the driver and my Babai settled into their seats, we were off.

"You must be hungry, Anni. Pinni has made some snacks for you. Amma told me that you love Pabbillalu and Murukulu," he said as he offered me an opened tin container of deep-fried rice flour chips.

"Thanks, Babai!" I said as I munched on the flavor-packed rice chips, "Oh my god, these are so good! Amma also makes these back home."

"Driver Uncle, please, take some snacks. You also must be tired. It is four in the morning!" I said as I handed the container to the driver, "I can promise you that you have never tasted Murukulu like these!" He chuckled before taking one himself.

"You're right. Even my wife does not make snacks like this, don't tell her I said that," he responded as he crunched on the snacks and winked at me through the mirror as I smiled back at him before turning my attention back to my uncle.

"Tell me, Babai, what's new?" I asked.

"Well, not much has changed since you spoke to us before you got on the plane. How are Amma, Nana, and your brother Saish doing?" he asked.

"They're all fine; nothing new there. I honestly cannot tell you how excited I am to be able to see everyone after six years. The last time I was here, I was fifteen. So much has happened, and even though I call and talk to all of you, I feel like I have missed so much."

"And that's why you're here. You have an entire trip ahead of you to make up for all you have missed. Don't think you are the only one who feels that way. We missed seeing you grow up too. Just look at you, all grown up. We all couldn't be prouder of the young woman you are today." he said, holding up my chin. "That's why everyone is excited when any of you come home," he said, as he gave me a soft smile.

After a moment of silence, he turned to me. "I am going to close my eyes for a bit, don't hesitate to wake me up if you need anything. You should also sleep. I don't know how much you slept on the plane ride here. I know that the car isn't very comfortable but try and get some rest at least. Everyone is eagerly waiting for you at home, and they won't let you rest once we reach," he said as I smiled. "We'll stop and get breakfast in an hour or two," he said as he pressed his head against the tattered seat and dozed off. I closed my eyes and rested my head against the window as I breathed in the organic air that flooded into the car.

I looked out the window, thinking of all the cousins who grew up before I had a chance to hold them, the grandparents I had only met once or twice before they left for a place they would never return from, and the memories I hadn't had the opportunity to make with my family. You're here now; make the most of it, I reminded myself as I opened my eyes and watched the streets pass by. There was a certain moment when the city's atmosphere faded away and was replaced by the incense of earthy roads that lay beneath and a sense of calmness not found in the city.

It was around six in the morning now, and the villages

and towns we passed through slowly came to life. Mothers in nightgowns ran back and forth, trying to pack lunches for their husbands and children while they tackled a tangled mess of their daughter's long hair, trying to tie it up into braids for school. The fresh morning was filled with chatter as some eyed our vehicle that passed by. I found it interesting how even though my parents immigrated to America twenty-three years ago, my mornings had been filled with the similar bustling I observed through the window. My mom, who I called Amma, always woke up before the rest of us, took a shower, and completed her Pooja before dragging my brother and I out of bed. As my brother and I got ready for school, she would make a steaming hot cup of coffee for my dad, prepare a hearty breakfast, and would pack lunches for all of us while we ran around trying to find everything for the day. After all of us left for school and my dad went to work, she would make herself a cup of coffee and would sit in her favorite chair near the window that overlooked our garden. I smiled to myself as I waved to the children, who reminded me of my younger self.

As we passed by the villages, One woman who stood in a brightly colored saree caught my eye as she reached for a broom and swept the dust that had accumulated overnight in front of her doorstep. She scooped her hands into a copper vessel and splattered water all over the surface, and then began. Bending down, she scooped white flour into her hand and slowly released small amounts to form a pattern of dots. She then looped the dots into families by drawing lines between them. As she stepped away, a larger pattern emerged; she began to smile. It wasn't the first time I had seen someone draw this pattern of dots and lines. My mom would create similar designs with a piece of chalk whenever we celebrated festivals such as Diwali. Amma had explained to me that the ritual of drawing a muggu in front of a home every morning was a symbol of family.

"No matter how far one dot is from another, it will always be looped into the pattern. Remember, no matter how far you venture, those lines of relationships you build will always tie you to this family." she had said to me. On trips to India, my own muggu would expand with every new relative I met; the lines connecting me to known relatives strengthened. However, just as a muggu fades, so did my relationships with my family. On leaving day, I would wipe away my tears, making empty promises to keep in touch and call every week. Each empty promise worked as an eraser on the lines I had built with my family. I felt tears well up in my eyes before I caught the driver's glance in the mirror and smiled back.

"Everything ok? You look deep in thought," he said.

"Ya, Uncle, I'm just tired from my journey," I said, trying to keep a steady voice as he smiled a little.

"My younger daughter is in sixth grade. She wants to grow up and go somewhere foreign like you!" he said in Telugu. "Maybe in a couple of years, I will be picking her up from the airport, taking her home," he said as I watched pride gleam in his eyes. I smiled and nodded, not knowing how to respond.

"I'm kind of hungry. Can we stop somewhere for breakfast?"

"There is a Dosa place nearby. We can stop there. Wake your Babai; he must be hungry too. We started from home at midnight, and he was so eager to receive you at the airport he didn't sleep a wink." He said as he looked at him through the mirror.

At the Dhaba, the waiter brought me a hot plate of Dosa with a side of Sambar and Chutney. We were all hungry and ate in silence. Although the Dosas were not crispy enough, the Sambar too liquidy, and the Chutney too salty, I said nothing as I stuffed my mouth with something that could cure my hunger.

My mom's cooking, on the other hand, was perfect and was popular among my friends and guests. Every time someone sat down for a meal at my place, they always left with a protruding belly and never-ending praise for my mom's food.

"Do you like the Dosa?" My Babai asked.

"It's alright. But, never would I eat it like that!" I exclaimed as I pointed to the atrocity my Babai was committing. He tore a piece off the Dosa and dipped it into the sambar and then into the chutney before placing it in his mouth. In my eyes, this was the equivalent of eating fries dipped in a mix of ranch and ketchup.

"Oh, come on, this is the real secret to enjoying Dosa properly!" he responded, grinning as I vigorously shook my head.

"No, that's disgusting," I said as we shared a chuckle.

"Do you want a cup of coffee?" Babai asked me.

"I don't drink coffee," I said. The only exception to this was my mom's coffee. Every once in a while, she would make a special kind of filter coffee that tasted better than any drink Starbucks could ever brew up. Gosh, how much I missed her and her cooking. I had just completed my third year in college, and instead of going back home after finals, I decided to fly straight to India. I found tickets in the first week of June and quickly booked them. Before I knew it, I was sitting in an airplane, ready to fly half away across the world on my own. I was so glad that in a couple of weeks, my mom, dad, and brother would also be coming to India. It wasn't long before we drove into the village that resembled the one I had remembered visiting when I was younger.

Although Pantapalli had changed since the last time I was here, the village's spirit remained evergreen. The increase in rainfall in recent years has led to a successful crop year. Palm trees waved in the warm breeze of the mid-morning, and bright green rice paddies decorated small reservoirs of water. Nature seemed to welcome the monsoon season with a festivity of its own. Many of the small houses had been replaced by larger two-story concrete buildings that were painted vibrantly. Men in worn white shirts, lungis, a cotton cloth wrapped around the waist that extended to the ankle, and a towel wrapped around their heads walked on the side of the road herding their cows to their respective fields. The cows here did not Moo like they did back home; instead, they bellowed a long Ambaa as we drove past them. After a long journey, we finally arrived. The colorfully painted concrete house sat in the middle of our small farmland. To the right of the house was a small shed where the cows were housed.

As soon as the car drove up to the house, cousins came running out of the gates, flinged open the SUV doors, and tackled me into a hug. "We missed you so much! Welcome to India!" they said as they squeezed me tight. "I missed you all too!" I said as I threw my arms around them. Six years, I thought to myself, how did six years go by since the last time I was here? I had promised myself to never forget the memories, to never forget the relationships I spent a summer building. How many of those promises had I kept?

I stepped onto the concrete platform that surrounded the house and looked up to see an eager crowd, their warm smiles radiating down the walkway. As I walked toward the house,

Lilly, my aunt's dog, welcomed me with a loud "Woof Woof!". My aunt struggled to not fall over as Lilly rushed toward me and dragged my aunt with her.

"Lilly! How are you? I know, I know, I missed you too!" I exclaimed as she tackled me into a hug and gave me a wet kiss. I stood up and saw my grandparents, my Attas, Mamas, Annas, Akkas, Pinnis, Babai, and so many other family members standing in front of me, grinning. The ground had been decorated with a beautiful muggu that spelled out Welcome Home Anu!

The muggu had been drawn largely with flowers decorating the dots and lines. This time, no empty promises. I am the artist of my muggu. I will learn to redraw these lines and make them permanent. I thought to myself as I looked up to see my cousin approaching me with a plate in her hand. It was custom that anytime someone arrived from a long journey, they were to be welcomed into the home after an Aarati, a ritual where a camphor piece is set on fire and circled in front of someone, to get rid of Dhishti, the evil eye. After the Aarati had finished, I approached my grandparents and bowed in front of them, touching my fingers to their feet before moving my hands towards my eyes as they blessed me. A round of hugs was exchanged, and suitcases were unloaded from the car with the help of everyone around me. After taking a deep breath, I finally took a step inside the house that I would learn to call home. This was the beginning of my Indian Summer.

Oceantown

Songhan Pang

It is a Friday morning in June, and the water is rising fast in the island of Oceantown. Locals would tell you that they were stationed somewhere outside the Keys and Havana, which would theoretically make sense. The water was colored the murky, cloudy green that could only be the result of runoff sewage treatment plants and fossil fuel burning. But unlike the tourist hotspots that surround it, Oceantown will go under first. The water crept into crevices of gray concrete homes and funneled into the cracks of weary pavement long due for renovation. "As if the ocean had sneezed and left the snot to dry," one photographer thought before banishing the thought.

Any map would tell you that Oceantown did not exist. Which, in a sense, was true now.

The town wakes bright and early as it always does — partly to get a head start on the world and partly out of spite. Wooden boats tethered to outposts were now coated with grimy, smelly seaweed and the contents of the village dumpster; people stood scrubbing in knee-length rubber boots, soaked raincoats, and too much salt—from water or sweat or tears, who knew. They wrung the remnants of their hair and clothes and hopes out to dry on twine lines as far above sea level as possible. Young children sloshed small buckets out the house and locked their doors after their parents before rushing off to school. Still, the water opened the door and crept in uninvited.

Jordan wakes up and immediately wants to fall asleep again. Unlike many people in the town, she wakes up in a dry bed two hours later than most, cushioned by white alpaca fur blankets and the security that being the daughter of a mayor of anything, even a small town with fishing as the only thing it's got going, comes with. Today, her room walls are an enchanted forest. With bleary, half-opened eyes, she rolls over and stares at the vast canopies she had painstakingly stroked onto the ceiling. As she longs for the cool shade of a forest, she remembers the framed picture on her father's nightstand. Amidst a crowd of people dressed in colorful Hawaiian shirts, there he was — younger — and proudly cutting a red ribbon. There was the promise of a new beginning. There were also trees. Pretty ones even, like willow and magnolia. "That's the town you're in right now," her father had told her multiple times. "You know, those rich big shots from higher up the East Coast used to stay here for multiple days before heading on their merry way to Mar-a-Lago. Took pictures and all that, too." Used to. Trees were just trees, and she figured it was only a matter of time until the loggers and Big Ag companies and miners discovered their hidden boon.

She did not think about how the water was rising. She did not think about school or the fact that she had stopped going. She did not think about Lev. Yes, definitely not Lev, who would do anything to win her father's annual fishing competition tonight, even if it meant missing time with her.

She hates fish — the way they look, smell, taste — but no one shared the sentiment or at least felt it necessary to communicate. But of course. Fish brings money. Fish would not make you question the day-to-day, monotonous, deteriorating life you live. No, fish would stare quietly at you; fish was at your mercy. It was as simple as that.

Painting, on the other hand.

For many days now, she has stayed in her room. Each day, she painted a different landscape to escape from the one she has been trapped in for fifteen years. Today, she thought about all the things that she told herself to not think about. How the fish in Oceantown were dwindling. How Lev and her were not the children they used to be. How the water was rising fast. Then, she prepared to paint them. She loves everything about painting —the way the brush is steady in her grip, the way she can blend beautifully different colors to form her own complex story. Painting was her way to make sense of the world. Yes, that was it. She dragged herself out of bed, grabbed the nearest bucket of cerulean blue paint, and threw it forcefully onto the wall. Droplets of ocean splashed and bled into the forest floor until there was nothing left. Today, she would paint the ocean. She would try to understand.

By the time she finished her masterpiece, the fishing competition had long been canceled. The water had risen to her windowsill. She would later explain that she knew it was coming. She held the memories of her painting close. She had finally begun to accept the life that had been thrust upon her. She only wished that more people had seen it before the waves had washed it away.

Samuel Davis will soon turn seventy-two. He remembers when Oceantown used to be a forest when it was not called Oceantown but something entirely different. He couldn't remember that. It wasn't important, anyways. Sometimes, the floods got so large that the entire town might as well be a drop in the ocean itself. Eventually, it will evaporate and turn into nothing. Deep down, he knew this was Oceantown's fate. The mayor's daughter seemed to understand it well enough, and that irked him. What did she know? The years had gone on, and the fish never left. They were the only thing he had left. Perhaps this was why the shore was packed every end of June, when the tide was the highest, when the fish were the most abundant. In small towns like these, a thrill is needed to keep dragging the inevitable along.

He was talented at fishing. Other fishermen remembered him as the old man who sported rubber gloves, rubber boots, rubber everything. Back in the late 20th century, when he was trying to make Morgan stay with him—please, just a few more years—the businesses and governance and structure in the town had only just started to form. Alas, he had the patience and solitude fit for a successful fisherman, earning him equally great deals of respect and frustration. He lived alone at the very base of the town near the docks and only arose to sit in a full gear of fishing PPE from sunrise until sundown, waiting for the returns that he had been deprived of all his life. He caught some and wanted more. In the beginning, after the gaping hole Morgan had left behind, a few naive boys had come up to his spot on the docks, poking and prodding the old man to their own detriment. It soon became evident that he had little hope in the younger generations to see the importance of his craft, and so no one dared approach him lest they be subject to his sour tempers. No one knew how old he was. He was a fixture like the rotting structures of the village homes and surplus of things that no one else in the world wanted.

Days before the fishing competition commenced and the water started rising, the rest of the townspeople had seen him taking walks around town, not sitting where he used to be. As the helicopters descended, they found his body floating in the middle of it all. But there were too many people to save, too many testimonials to be snatched, and so he was forgotten. By the time the rescue squad remembered, his body had already followed the current and tipped over the orange horizon.

The rescuers came in waves. Oceantown was between the Keys and Havana, but not near either, so someone must have done something right and shared their location with whoever was out there. When the helicopter came, it flew at least a mile away before sputtering, turning back around, and hovering just above the sunken town. Oops, almost missed ya there! A young woman in her early twenties with white-blond hair stuck her head out of the doorway and smiled apologetically, waving a perfectly manicured hand and promising more reinforcements. The people held onto rooftops and the sides of flimsy boats or makeshift ones in response, wet and shivering from the cold wind gusting from the helicopter blades and too tired to say anything. Their mayor managed to stand up shakily and wave back in acknowledgment. In the light, his hair looked just a little less grayer than it actually was.

Lev curled his knees closer to his chest and wanted to laugh at the horror of it all. This was hour 15 of being awake and counting.

He had never been as physically strong as the other kids, but he had always been more patient and alert. Tonight could have been the night that he would have won and proved to the town that he and Aimee were more than just the poor children whose mother was washed away by that flood years ago. He gripped his hand tighter to his boat until his knuckles turned white and tried not to cry.

"Lev, where's Jordan?" Aimee asked from across him, her blue eyes wide with worry. Her pink t-shirt was nearing a drab brown, and her teeth chattered loudly. He sighed and pulled her closer to him. She didn't deserve any of this. None of them did.

"In her house," he reassured her, "don't worry, she's safe." He looked up at the only two-story building in the vicinity, now reduced to a lone floating white block. He felt rather than knew that she was in her room as always. Perhaps it was the way her hair always looked drier than his, her backpack sharp and new, her brown eyes bored with fate. Anyways, we'll go underwater by 2030 and not 2040 like our next-door neighbors, so y'all better start swimming, she had proclaimed. Must be nice to be able to see Oceantown from above.

If Jordan had looked out her window, she would have seen this: a smooth mass of shimmering blue, deceptively calm and reflecting the dying sun, only disturbed by splotches of drab hues. If you did not look carefully, each splotch could have easily been a piece of floating trash.

Now, zoom out of that view. Keep going. Don't stop. That's what the helicopters saw.

The news spread. In Maine, a woman and her mother watched NBC South Florida. "What's that?"

"It's the news, Mom. On what happened in Oceantown."

"What's Oceantown?"

"Apparently, it's an island in the middle of the Gulf of Mexico? Looks like the water's been rising real bad there, and the whole island the town was on finally gave out." "...Oh."

"Yeah."

"..."

"…"

"What? You look a little pale, Mom. Are you okay? This is all really scary, I know. And we're on the coast, too. Do you think this'll happen to us one day? We wake up, and the entire world is just water? Ugh, it's so terrible to think about."

"Yes. Perhaps. I don't know. It's just…"

"Just?"

"It didn't used to be called that."

"Oh."

"Yes…yes. But let's keep watching."

After the helicopters had come and the people had been pulled out of the water, after Jordan had left the comforts of her room after the reporters had parked outside the hospital (but not before planning the day excursion to the Keys), Mr. Johnson, the mayor of Oceantown, woke up with a start, eyes bloodshot and heavy. Even a rare night's worth of sleep could not quell his mixed emotions now. He knew it was trivial to worry about a fishing competition when your entire town was underwater, but he couldn't help it. He remembers sitting by Jordan's bedside late at night, trying to tell her his truth: "I know you don't like this town, Jordan. I know. And I know your mom would want to go back to the States, too. But please understand that the people in this town have stood the test of time. Even rocks in an ocean will eventually erode and scatter into sand. We need something to bring us together, to make us feel that we belong with the rest of the world. Fishing isn't just a pastime, not always. It's a matter of our survival." She had pulled the covers up to her ears and asked for space. He gave her that and now wondered if he gave too much. She loves painting and not fishing, and he was mostly happy about that.

Beep…. Beep…. Beep. His head feels like a bowling ball lolling around on his neck as he struggles to sit up. Where was Jordan? Memories from the day before flood him in a rush. The water rising, the hasty town center, the getting of townspeople onto rooftops and into boats, calling the first in a list of numbers for moments like these, calling Jordan but getting left on voicemail, panicking, exhaustion, blackout. Where was Jordan?

Beep .. Beep .. Beep. He frantically searches for the button to call the nurse, but she was there before he could lift a finger.

"Sir, please calm down. You must be worried about your daughter, but I'd like you to know that she's well and is finishing up an interview with the reporters outside. You must be proud to have such a mature daughter that represents your town so well."

Slowly, he laid back down. Later, when the nurses had left him alone in his room, he would turn on the television to find his daughter mournfully staring back at him on NBC 6 South Florida. He would see the pictures of the remnants of his town, which was not a town anymore, not in a physical sense. His people, on the other hand, were not remnants. He knew this to be true — not from the aerial view photographs that said otherwise, but from his own eyes with everyone else at sea level. He would go to sleep with the thought of old Samuel Davis and the strange strength of tragedy and memory to bring people together. In the morning, he would find his daughter. He would find his people, be a listening ear. Then, he would start the process of healing.

Any map would tell you that Oceantown did not exist. This, in a sense, is still true, but not by her watch. She takes up her brush for the first time in a long time and makes the first stroke.

Brood X

Jayne Ogilvie-Russel

The day I get the news, the first thing I feel is selfish. Why, I don't quite know. It's mid-May, the night air unseasonably hot, an auspice of the feverish summer yet to come. I'm sitting on the porch, nursing a lemonade-like fine wine. It's cool against my lips, though my body is warm; sweat coats me like a second skin, its residue smeared along the crystal glass. A thin dusting of yellow-green blankets every flat surface for miles; I trace patterns through it with my right hand, breaking up the clumps of pollen.

It's 2021, which means it's the year of Brood X. I'm watching a cluster of cicadas climb up a column as if it were a tree, unable to tell the difference. It's slow work; their abdomens throb in the heat as they inch their way to the top, looking for a place to molt. Some of them have already begun to shed their skins, like a Xenomorph bursting out in slow-motion, their green bodies dangling from their perch, their new shells still soft and dewey. There are a few empty skins littering the column like little brown ghosts. I reach forward and pluck one off. It's wafer-thin in my palm, and I listen to the quiet crunch as my fingertips grind it into powder, letting the flakes fly off like ash in the breeze.

Behind me, the door opens, and yellow light floods the porch. My mom steps out. The first thing I notice is her face, tart as a lemon, her lips twisted and quirked to the side. She has her phone in her hands, and as she moves to sit next to me, she sets it on the porch. "Doug had a stroke." She says. Her tone is completely neutral.

"Our Doug, or Doug from church?" Is the first thing out of my mouth.

"Our Doug."

"Oh." For a moment, silence screams like a banshee.

"How did it happen?" I finally ask. "Is he going to be okay?"

She sighs, shakes her head. "He was on a call with his boss. She noticed his face drooping. The doctors don't know what caused it. He hasn't woken up."

"Will he?"

"Hopefully."

We drop it after that, staring off into the nascent-summer night. My eyes are watching the cicadas, hers the liriope swaying in the breeze. My father's car pulls into the driveway, and it takes the loud slam of its door for me to notice. He steps out with his briefcase and walks over to the porch, bending down to plant a kiss on Mom's cheek.

"Your brother had a stroke," she tells him.

"I know." He says, "Barry called me."

"We should check in with your parents," She replies.

"I'll call. We'll have dinner with them this weekend."

"Not Friday. I have a meeting with a client, and Alex has to study."

"I'll let them know." He pushes his way into the house. I follow after, trailing him into the kitchen.

"I made dinner tonight," I say as he heaps roast zucchini into his bowl.

"Have you and Mom already eaten?"

"Yeah. We were hungry." He nods in response before he opens up the freezer and grabs the gin and a handful of ice cubes. They crackle under the fizz of tonic water as he pours, topping off the glass with a splash of grapefruit juice.

"It's a Wednesday," I say.

"I know." He replies.

He eats in the living room, and we don't talk. I grab my flashcards from the kitchen table and rejoin Mom on the porch. I spend the rest of the night cycling through the same ten terms, forgetting them each time.

Cult of Domesticity. Don't know, next. Seneca Falls Convention. Something-something feminism, next. Transcendentalism. Not sure, next.

It takes three days before we hear anything else. When we do, the news isn't good. "He's awake," my aunt says, voice a static blare from the speaker phone, "but they found a mass in his brain. They're going to have to do a special MRI."

She sends us a picture of the initial scan. Sure enough, there's a round dimple in the back, no larger than a penny. The conversation goes on a bit longer, but I'm not listening. I grab a dime from the coin bowl and walk out onto the porch. The cicadas have started their song now, and their buzz is almost deafening, a chorus 10,000 strong. I sit down, with the cacophony blasting in my ears, and I place the dime on my tongue, sucking on it, letting it scrape against my molars, gnash my teeth, press it to the roof of my mouth, focus on the tannic taste of metal so that I might think of anything else. A cicada bumbles about straight into my chest, clumsy as a carpenter bee, and grips onto my shirt. I shake it off, spit out the dime, and head back inside.

The next night, we visit my grandparents in their fifth-floor apartment in a retirement community for veterans and foreign service officers. We ride the one working elevator up to their floor and knock on their door. From inside comes a call and response of, "Ted, the door!" and "One moment, please!" We wait for a second before hinges squeak, and Poppy ushers us in.

Inside, the entrance smells like lemon and giggly water, as Grandi calls it. She's left her easter decorations up, pastel eggs, and fuzzy yellow chicks, and little rabbits arranged neatly on every countertop and windowsill. A big vase of canary roses rests on their coffee table, surrounded by a ring of condolence cards. The sound of sizzling meat trickles in from the kitchen.

"It's nice out, so we'll eat on the patio," Poppy informs us.

"Go help Grandi set the table," Mom tells me.

I grab the silverware from the drawer, then the printed napkins from the counter, and make my way outside to where my parents are sitting. The patio is nice: a concrete slab with a big glass table and some outdoor chairs, roofed with tin and surrounded by panels of netting. Even with the screens, a cicada has managed to get in; it screams from the ceiling, calling out to its brethren swarmed in the nearby trees. I set the cutlery down and sit right beneath it. Grandi shuffles in with a tray of chicken and cooked vegetables. We take turns passing tongs around the table, waxed paper plates gradually filling with food. Poppy is the first one to address the elephant in the room.

"Barry told us it's likely a tumor."

"Did she?" My dad responds. "I thought they didn't know the prognosis." "They don't. That's just her assumption, but I believe it. God only knows what radiation the Soviets were shooting at our embassy in Prague."

My stomach drops like a rock, and I no longer feel like eating, so I push the last remaining pieces of bell pepper around my plate like they're air hockey pucks, and I'm a particularly uncoordinated player.

Grandi clears her throat. "Douglas is going to be fine. He's in good hands." Her voice is pitched up in the fake-chipper tone she takes on whenever she's upset. "Let's discuss something else. Alex, how are your exams going?"

"They're fine," I respond. "APUSH is this Wednesday. Then Latin, then Lang. They're mostly online this year. I'm taking them from home."

The conversation shifts to something, something schools these days have way too many opportunities to cheat. I'm not really paying attention, stabbing a steamed potato with my fork. I excuse myself to go to the bathroom and spend 40 minutes sitting on the floor, staring up at its cicada-less ceiling. When I come out, my mom stage-whispers, "Are you alright?"

"I'm fine," I say. "Just indigestion." We go home not long after that.

For the next few days, I focus on nothing but my exams: flashcards, practice tests, study groups, more flashcards. On Wednesday, I sit at my desk in the sunroom with my knee bouncing up-down, up-down, and my fingers playing a frantic game of whack-a-mole with the keyboard. The exam shuts down with just enough time for me to finish the DBQ, and I'm left with a racing heart and a surge of adrenaline, strong and aching like a compressed coil. I grab my earbuds and sprint out the door, music blasting in my ears so loud I can't even hear the cicadas. I run down the street, feet slapping against the pavement, heel-toe, base booming in my ears louder than lions. I get tired after a block, walk for two minutes, sprint again, walk, sprint, walk, sprint. I run down the hill, into the woods, across the stream, and through the narrow path to a rope swing above the shallow waters of Pimmit Run, where I sit for an hour, not swinging, just sitting, staring out at the stream swirling just below, the rope digging into my hands, the seat digging into my thighs, but I don't care because this is the best I've felt all week. Eventually, my mom calls, and my trance is disturbed. The loud blare of the ringtone interrupts the crescendo of my song; Siri butchers my mom's last name. I pick up on the second ring.

"Where did you wander off to?" My mom asks.

"I'm at the creek," I reply.

"I'm going to go check in with the crew at the Fowler's. Take the dogs on a walk when you get back home, alright?"

"Will do." I hang up and consider staying another hour, but the moment has fled. I plod back home to the song of the cicadas and take the dogs on a walk. Pippin jumps in the air to eat every bug she passes. Blossom snarfles along the ground. I try to drag them away, but both end up eating so many cicadas they gag, hacking up half-digested wings and bits of shell.

Thursday evening, my dad takes us out to ice cream. The weather is gorgeous: 70 degrees and sunny, the evening sun still high in the sky. I've been stressing over my Latin exam all day, poring over passage translations and verb conjugations. I'm explaining the difference between a gerund and a gerundive to my mom when Dad clears his throat and turns to face me from the passenger seat.

"Barry called this afternoon. It's cancer."

I swallow dry air. "What type? Stage?"

"Glioblastoma. Stage four." He says, voice completely steady.

"Is it malignant? Is there anything they can do?"

"He's going to have surgery to remove the tumor, then chemo and radiation. One of the best neurologists in Massachusetts is going to do the operation," he says in consolation.

"Okay," I say, and go back to explaining the facets of Latin grammar to my mom. On my phone, I'm rapidly searching "glioblastoma studies, glioblastoma life expectancy, glioblastoma can you live with it?" Mayo Clinic does nothing to assuage my fears.

We get to the ice cream shop, and I order, but I only eat two bites of the mango-pineapple punch before I sit down next to my dad with my dessert beside me, and my breath shaky. It doesn't feel right to be indulging amidst a family member's slow decline. My dad pats my back warmly, but it only makes me want to eat even less because I don't know what I'd do without him, and I can't imagine what my cousin must be going through.

We go home, and I go to bed early, partly because I have a test tomorrow, partly because I'm exhausted, and partly because I just want the day to end.

Despite my hopes, Friday is just as fraught. I take the test, this one in-person, held in the small reading room off the end of my High School's library, and though I'm distracted, I feel decent about my performance. Both my parents pick me up when I finish, and once more, in the car, they deliver bad news.

My father's former business partner had a son, age fifteen, who, this Monday, died of a brain tumor he struggled with for the vast majority of his life. The funeral, a small gathering of friends and family, is going to be held this Saturday. I feel conflicted about going; I hadn't known him well, nor did I know his family, but my father did, and I knew it was important for us to be present.

"I'm so sorry to hear that," I say, but my words feel hollow, and my gut feels tighter than a well-fitted dovetail hinge.

We drive home in silence.

The next day, we wake up early and load into the car with plenty of time to make the 9 am service in Annapolis, Maryland. We pull in 40 minutes early, just outside the church, and camp out on the patio of a Starbucks while we wait for more people to arrive. My suit is a bit stuffy, but there's a breeze from the water, and the cicadas are close to silent on Mainstreet.

At 8:45, we file into the pews. The church is an old building with stained glass mosaics and a high, vaulted ceiling. Between the decorative molding of the pillars, the vault is painted a deep royal blue, gilded with tiny golden stars. I stare at the ceiling until the service starts, eyes unmoving.

9:00 sharp, the family shuffles in with the coffin's procession. We all stand, sing a hymn, and sit down. The priest begins by reading scripture, something about finding solace in the Lord. He moves into his sermon, asking us not to grieve but to celebrate a life lived with strength and compassion, that everything happens for a reason, that God has a plan for all. Midway through his speech, I hear a buzzing to my left. I look over to see a cicada smashing itself into a nearby window, bonking its head repeatedly as if, this time, it will be able to escape. The priest finishes speaking, and my father's coworker takes the pulpit with his wife and daughter. The three of them look tired; their eyes are rimmed with red. They share anecdotes about their son, their brother, how he never stopped fighting, how he was always so positive, even when he spent more time at the hospital than he did at home, even when he lost his eyesight, even when he was wracked with such splitting migraines that he would be bedridden for days. In the corner, the cicada starts chirping. I feel tears well in my eyes, but I don't cry.

A few more people get up to speak. We take communion, and we are allowed to, even though we aren't Catholic. The reception is held outside, in the garden, where the cicadas are loud, and I stand awkwardly in a corner, just observing. We leave after an hour and a half as the rest of the guests are trickling out. I'm glad to go home.

Sunday comes, then Monday, Tuesday, Wednesday. I take my last exam, feel okay about it. Time seems to flow like chewing gum, slow, sticky, ballooning, then bursting in an instant. When it happens, it's Thursday. I'm sitting on my bed reading a beat-up copy of The Things They Carried for class. Sun is streaming through my window, and my room is getting hot. I have a fan blasting in the corner, a furious whir. I turn the crinkled, yellow page, and my stomach catches in my throat. The protagonist is describing the regrets of his life, the people that he sees when he flees across the river into Canada, dodging the draft. Among them is a girl, still young, and he reflects on how she was the first person he ever lost. She died of a brain tumor.

I throw the book across my room, and it slams into my bookshelf with a loud thud. My breath picks up, harsh and uneven. My fingers grasp for purchase on my arms, sliding up-down, up-down, nails digging into my skin. They chafe as they scratch, tingly like needles poking into my pores, but at least it's a sensation. At least it isn't spiraling. For a minute, I stay hunched on my bed, my breaths sharp. Soon, it becomes too much. I'm hot, I feel trapped, I feel enclosed, I need to get out. With my fingers still digging into my arms, I run down the stairs and out the back door, scramble up the hill and sit beneath the towering cedar in our yard, half-dead of some fungal disease but still a patchy green. I rock back and forth with the rhythm of the breeze. I don't realize I'm crying until I feel dew on my cheeks, and it feels almost scalding because this is the first time I've cried in years. Above me, I'm startled by the buzz of a cicada, as grating as cutting styrofoam. I look up and see it climbing the tree. I stare at its bulbous form, throbbing in the heat, its blood-red eyes, its wings like crumpled plastic. My stomach roils. I feel like gagging. The cicada screams and screams, and I wish that it would shut up—please, shut up—so that I can have just a moment of quiet, of peace, a moment of room to think about anything else other than the fact that we spend so much of our lives wasted underground, hiding from the world, hiding from our loved ones, hiding from ourselves, and by the time we emerge and metamorphosize and realize our truth our time is gone, or close to gone; we sing, we fuck, we die, without enough time to even see the fruits of our labor, because that's what the cicada does, that's what the cicada is, a species with the shortest end of the evolutionary stick; its strategy to be so prolific that it doesn't matter if one, or a hundred, or a million of its kind get eaten, or crushed, or fly off into the sun because there are still enough of them to blanket the trees and the ground and reproduce with enough cicada babies to start the 17-year cycle of futility all over again.

They don't do it for a reason.

There is no reason.

Things don't happen for a reason.

There is no reason for the cicada to be snatched off of the tree. There is no reason for thumbs to press down against its head and abdomen, still throbbing. There is no reason for a sickening crack to ring out into the air, like the sound of knuckles popping and globs of hemolymph to splatter, sticky, onto a pair of hands. There is no reason for its wings to be torn off, a quick one-two, popping out of their sockets before they're scattered like ash in the breeze. There is certainly no reason for the cicada to be brought up to a pair of lips, shoved between gnashing teeth, and swallowed like a coin, except the coin was spit out, so swallowed very much unlike a coin. There is no reason for me to sit against the tree, breathing harshly, eating a cicada. And yet I am. I swallow, but the nuttiness of its meat still coats my tongue, sickeningly sweet. It makes me want to throw up, but instead, I just sob.

I sob and feel selfish and hate that I know why.

Elle

Natalie Baumeister

I need to stop thinking about the blood on my shoes because it makes me nauseous, and I need to appear calm for Elle's sake. Breathe.

Elle is at her best friend's house for a birthday sleepover. There are enough pink balloons and streamers in the front yard to cover several parade floats, and I want to laugh at the absurdity, but laughing might lead to sobbing. Elle throws a tantrum when I force her to leave. The other eight-year-olds watch us with wide eyes on their frosting-smeared faces as I drag Elle to the car. There's no way I'm telling her about her dad's death.

Elle, now exhausted from her howling and flailing, pouts in the back seat, glaring out the window with her arms crossed. The unicorn on her pajamas grins at me in the reflection of the window as if the party hasn't ended and my world isn't crumbling.

"This car is gross," Elle grumbles.

In the backseat, on the side where Elle isn't sitting, a sticky patch of soda coats the upholstery. When I drove Elle home from school yesterday, she begged me to buy her a soda. I knew her parents wouldn't approve of it, but we swung by McDonald's, and I got her what she wanted. I told her it would be our little secret; our mischievous colludings were one of the reasons she preferred me to all her previous nannies. Then I immediately hit a speed bump, and Elle spilled soda over my backseat and herself. I was embarrassed. Her mom was livid. Her dad laughed at me for five minutes straight, which at that point was more mocking than genuine humor.

Earlier today, after dropping Elle off at the party, I went to get my car cleaned, only to discover that I'd left my wallet on my dresser. I made the long drive back to Elle's home, where I'd been living for the past two years. As I pulled into the driveway, I noticed that the front door was open. I went inside to investigate, and when I found Liam, my sticky car wasn't my top priority anymore.

I grip the steering wheel so my hands don't shake. There was no time to process Liam's death. I'm not sure if I want to process it or if I can.

We are the only car on the highway. The clouds obscure any starlight, and the streetlamps are spaced so far apart that they're useless. My headlights stretch into unending darkness as if I'm traveling through an abyss.

The dark used to be Elle's greatest fear years before I was hired. She didn't trust her other nannies, so if her night light burned out or a storm took out the power, she would go to Liam's room and shake him awake. He would make up stories to keep her mind off her fear, and once she fell asleep again, he would carry her to her room and tuck her into bed.

She'll never see him again. He'll never tell her stories or tuck Elle into bed, or—I try swallowing the bile burning my throat, but my stomach is in knots, and my lunch won't stay down. I slam on the brake. My seat belt catches me as I fly forward, smacking my chest. Elle shrieks, but I can't apologize because if I open my mouth, vomit will spew across the dashboard.

I open my door and lean out of the car into a cold wind, my chest aching where the seat belt pulls against me. I throw up on the road.

"Ew, Annie!" says Elle. She knows I hate that nickname, but I don't have the energy to care right now.

My mouth tastes bitter. I need time to catch my breath, but every minute I spend hanging out of this car is wasted. I close the door then accelerate.

"Sorry," I pant. "Are you okay?"

"I want to go to Sierra's." A curtain of hair blocks her face in the mirror. It's red and curly like Liam's.

The last time I saw Liam, his hair stuck to the blood dripping from the hole in his head. I swerve. My hands are clammy, and I wish they could reach into my mind and pull out the memory or claw out my eyes, just like Oedipus in the story that gave me nightmares when I was Elle's age. A cornfield appears beside the road. The crops extend into the void of the horizon, where the distant silhouettes of corn husks almost look like blades. "You'll see Sierra later," I lie. Who knows when Elle's life returns to normal? "Where are we going?"

"It's a surprise." Not just for her but for me too. When I discovered blood dripping down Liam's wallpaper, I almost called the police, but I'm no longer naive enough to trust them, so I dialed his wife's number instead. Candace is out of the country for a business trip, but she answered immediately, and once I explained everything, she told me to rush to Elle before "they" got her too. I asked who she meant, but she just gave me an address for where I should take Elle. A "safe house." She ordered me to break my phone so I couldn't be tracked, then hung up. In a whirlwind of panic, I threw my phone against the wall, and glass and plastic and computer chips shattered into Liam's blood, and holy shit, the police might use the debris as evidence that I hurt him.

"When will we be there?" asks Elle.

"Soon."

She sticks up her sharp chin. Liam does—did—that whenever he saw something unpleasant on the news. "I hate when grown-ups say that." Her green eyes glare at my reflection—Liam's eyes.

My chest constricts.

Breathe. Focus on the road. Ignore Liam. Think about anything other than Liam. My headlights cast a ghostly glow on the corn. Somewhere beyond this sea of yellow is our sanctuary. But what about Liam's sanctuary? Where was Candace when he needed her the most? Really though, where is Candace? It seems like she goes on a business trip at least once a month, and neither she nor Liam has ever told me where she travels. Last year,

Candace arrived home from the airport, and when I picked up her dropped passport, she snatched it from me and shoved it in her pocket before rushing her luggage to her bedroom. Despite my curiosity, I didn't ask questions. Barely anyone wants to hire a college dropout, much less provide one with a free room and meals, so I didn't want to give Candace a reason to fire me. I wouldn't have been hired if the couple wasn't so desperate for someone who had the patience for Elle's tantrums.

"Mom and Dad will be mad that you took me away from the party," she grumbles. Tears prick my eyes. "Your mom told me to get you." I wipe my eyes on my sleeve. "You're lying, Diannie." She kicks my seat. "I'm telling Mom and Dad." I want to rebuke her for kicking, but my words are caught in my throat. What will happen when I tell her that she'll never speak to her dad again?

Another engine rumbles on the road behind us. The car has its headlights off. My skin prickles, and my stomach twists. I want to believe that there are lots of reasons why the car wouldn't have its headlights on in the middle of the night and why it's accelerating, but the only explanation that makes sense is the one that I'm too terrified to consider.

A gunshot shakes the air, and it's like a bolt of electricity shoots through me. Elle presses her hands and face against the window. "I don't see the fireworks." Dread seeps through me, and my throat is dry, and my racing heart hurts my chest, and we're on an open highway that stretches for miles, and there's no way Elle and I can escape. This cornered animal feeling is one I know well, despite my efforts to forget it. Like when the police broke down the door to my apartment during my sophomore year in college and arrested me for the murder of my neighbor. Half-asleep and twice as afraid, I staggered into the flashing red and blue lights of police cars, then wide awake and terrified into a cell smaller than my bathroom. I still don't know how my DNA ended up on my neighbor or how I slept through his brutal demise. I wasted months in jail, and each day the dread of my impending trial date augmented the suffocating feeling of being a mouse moments before the cat pounces. But I dodged the predator's claws. A lawyer worth the rest of my tuition money got me out on a technicality but didn't prove my innocence. With my finances and emotions drained, I couldn't return to college, and I had hoped that entering childcare would bring me joy and comfort. But now, a little girl's father is dead, and we could be next.

I jerk the car off the road and into the cornfield. There's so much corn crunching under my wheels and thumping against the windows, and my hands ache from clenching the steering wheel, but I can't relax my fingers and the other car is following us, and Elle is screaming, and I tell her to stay calm, but she doesn't stop her banshee howl, and I can't think because all I can see is corn slamming against the windshield and all I can hear is Elle wailing—"Shut up!" I snap.

She flinches and sinks into the seat. A pang of guilt stabs my heart, but it's not the time for apologies.

They get closer. I've made a trail for them, and my headlights are their beacon. Shit. I switch off the lights.

We plunge into terrifying darkness. The corn stalks are dark shadows attacking the car. Elle screams again, and I want to screech so hard I tear my vocal cords, but I can't. I can't let Elle know how scared I am.

"Elle, it'll be okay." My voice wavers.

"Diana, I want Mom and Dad," she whines.

The other car flips on its headlights, and I flinch and squint in the glaring brightness. I was stupid to think we could escape through the corn. Elle's teary face gazes at me in the mirror. A face that's so much like Liam's. They may share the same eyes and freckles and nose, but they won't share the same bullet holes.

"Elle, I need you to listen, okay?"

She grips her seat belt. "What's going on?"

My heart races. "I'm going to stop the car, and you'll need to run."

"No!"

I take a shaky breath. "Just run. Don't wait for me."

Her eyes widen. "Are you coming?"

"I'll drive the car away. They'll follow me. I'll find you later."

Abandoning a child in a dark, chilly cornfield is a god-awful idea, but it'll make it harder for these people to find her. Hell, even I don't know how I'll find her, but I'll deal with it after we make it out of this cornfield alive.

"No." She stifles a sob.

"You'll be safe."

She hugs herself. "I don't wanna be alone."

"Elle, you need to be brave." My eyes are wet. "I love you. Your parents love you." Warm tears fall down my cheeks. I don't want her to know I'm scared, but I don't have time to dry my face.

"I want them," she sobs. "I want Mom and Dad."

"You'll see them if you run. Run through the corn. Whatever you hear or see, don't stop running."

"But—"

"Elle," I snap. My heart wrenches. "You need to run."

Another gunshot. My stomach contorts, but I have nothing left to throw up. "Elle? Do you understand?"

"Yes," she says softly.

I lick my lips. "What will you do?"

"Run."

"Good." My pulse reverberates in my skull. "I'm stopping the car now. Get ready." I slam on the brakes, and we skid to a stop. Corn bounces against the windshield, hammering a chaotic drumbeat. My heartbeat shakes my body.

Elle tugs at the door. "It's stuck."

The other car gets closer, and my skin tingles.

"Other door," I say.

Elle slides to the other side of the car, forgetting to avoid the soda stain, and opens the door. She looks at me, her face shiny with tears and snot.

"Run," I snap. My face is just as wet as hers.

She gasps and gets out of the car. She slams the door shut then runs into the corn, her small figure swallowed in the night. Holy shit, I hope this is the right move. It's hard to breathe, but I have to go. I slam my foot on the pedal, and the engine roars. My car cuts through corn—

Gunshot. I flinch. My car sinks to the right. They shot my wheel, but I'm still moving, even if the ride is bumpy and I'm veering to the side. Glass from the rear window sprays across the backseat as a bullet whizzes past my ear and through the windshield. Another bullet cracks my side mirror, and another bang and my car is sinking and slowing to a snail's crawl.

"No, no, no." I slam my foot on the accelerator, and the car shakes but doesn't go any faster. They shot a second wheel. "Shit!" The world spins around me. Every shadowy corn stalk blends into a monster prepared to devour me.

But it won't eat Elle.

My hand trembles as I open my door. The chilly wind nips at my face, and I shiver in my thin jacket. My legs are unsteady as I stumble out of the car onto uneven ground. I've barely taken two steps before I trip over fallen corn. My face slams into the soil, sending a shot of pain through my skull. I want to cry and scream.

White headlights grow bigger, blinding me. My body shakes, but I manage to stand. I run.

Corn stalks whip my face and scratch my arms. It's claustrophobic. I've never felt terror like this before, an all-consuming fear that grasps me and squeezes me in its fist. My head aches, and my legs are sore, but stopping means dying.

Bullets hit metal—they're shooting up my car, and these gunshots are more of a sharp pop than gunshots in movies, and if I weren't panting for breath, I would laugh because Liam loves spy movies—loved spy movie—even the cheesy ones, and he thought the people with guns were so badass, and because he admired them, Elle admired them, but guys with guns aren't as awesome to them now, and I'll never watch another spy or cop movie, and now everything spins and blurs around me, and the vast darkness engulfs me, and maybe I'm screaming, and the car gets closer, and all this damn corn looks the same, and I don't know where I am, and Elle is alone feeling this same horror.

Lights brighten the plants ahead of me. The car is right behind me.

Corn explodes with a bullet beside me. A burst of adrenaline blasts through me. I race faster.

More bullets fly. It's difficult to breathe between gasping for air and struggling with tears. Everything hurts. I'd give anything to rest.

A gunshot booms across the cornfield, and I'm falling forward. My knees hit the ground then my nose grinds into the dirt. It's a millisecond of nothing before pain flares in me, burning my back with the wrath of hell. I cry out and gasp, sucking soil into my mouth. It's rough and bitter, and I spit it out, the motion sending another wave of anguish through my body. My stomach twists, and my chest constricts. This is the most agonizing pain of my life. Fingers of fire extend across my flesh, stabbing me like an army of needles. Blood warms my skin, and my face is slick with tears.

My heart races like I just finished a marathon. But this isn't the finish. It can't be. I press my hands into the soil where corn husks and pebbles dig into my palms, and I try pushing myself up. A fiery spike of pain bolts through my body. I groan, and my chest hits the ground. The car stops, and people get out.

I grit my teeth and push against the ground, straining my arms, but I can't pull myself up. My legs won't move. They're numb.

"Fuck!" My tears fall into the dirt. I should've driven faster. I should've run harder. I should've done so many things differently, better, but I didn't. Now I'm fucked. I'm hollow. The pit in my stomach is deep and dark, like the black abyss around me. I can't escape either. Is this how Liam felt? No, they got him in the head, so he must have died instantly. Did he see his killers coming? Did he run away in a panicked frenzy? His green eyes peer at me through the corn, our killers' headlights gleaming in them. Am I on the bridge to the afterlife? No. This is too much pain to be dead. I must be hallucinating because of the blood loss.

My jacket is heavy with blood. I bought it a few months ago because I was desperate for a last-minute jacket and this was the cheapest option. Elle called it the most hideous thing she ever saw, so of course, I wore it constantly to make her cringe. It was so stupid. My ironically poor fashion choices were stupid, my petty sense of humor was stupid, and all this pain is stupid.

Liam's eyes aren't stupid. They're miserable. Terrified. Maybe in the afterlife, I'll look at his eyes and be met with repugnance because I couldn't save Elle.

But those aren't his eyes…

They're Elle's.

It's another bone-shattering punch from the universe. I led these people right to her. I'm sobbing harder, and the bullet hole in my back burns while I cry, but I can't help it. "Run," I mouth.

Her green eyes blur into the shadows. Everything melds into a swatch of gray and navy then monstrous figures surround me.

The bullet barely hurts anymore. Most of the pain is in my chest, like an animal inside is clawing at my flesh. Colors swirl and fade. There's so much I wanted to do with my life. Footsteps crunch behind me. Someone hovers over me. His presence makes my skin tingle, and one last bout of nausea racks me.

Gunshot.

St. Augustine's Monster and the Disappearance of the Spray

Matthew Kern

In 1896, an unexplainable mass of flesh belonging to a yet unknown creature appeared on the shores of Anastasia Island. The mass had no organs and was bereft of any defining features which might allow for identification. Its appearance first piqued the curiosity of local children before demanding the attention of the world's leading marine biologists. Professor Addison Verrill of Yale University wrote the following piece in the Sunday supplement of the New York Herald:

"The living weight of the creature was about eighteen or twenty tons. When living, it must have had enormous arms, each one a hundred feet or more in length, each as thick as the mast of a large vessel, and armed with hundreds of saucer-shaped suckers, the largest of which would have been at least a foot in diameter... Its eyes would have been more than a foot in diameter. It would have carried ten or twelve gallons of ink in the ink bag. It could swim rapidly, without doubt, but its usual habit would be to crawl slowly over the bottom of deep water in pursuit of prey...

"We must reflect that wherever this creature had its home, there must be living hundreds or even thousands of others of its kind, probably of equal size; otherwise, its race could not be kept up..." Time soon passed, and the mass' defiance against categorization led many to gloss over its existence rather than let it reform their conceptions of the ocean and its nature. Verrill himself eventually amended his statements, later claiming it was most likely some fragment of a sperm whale. It would turn out, however, that Verrill's initial musings held far more truth than he

114

might have realized, barring one important detail:

The creature would find its prey sailing across the open ocean.

In December of 1909, Joshua Slocum found himself sailing in the Bermuda Triangle, approximately 500 miles off the coast of Anastasia Island, where, thirteen years previous, a small fragment of molted flesh belonging to the St. Augustine's Monster had washed ashore. Slocum was a man of peerless maritime acumen, having single-handedly circumnavigated the globe in his sloop named The Spray. On November 14, 1909, Slocum set sail from Massachusetts with the intention of arriving in the West Indies. With Slocum's experience and fair weather ahead, nothing should have gone wrong.

A North wind filled the main and jib of The Spray, her boom hard to the starboard side and sheets nearly full out. The smashed face of Slocum's tin clock told him the hour was still young, and ahead was a full day of travel. The wafts of brine and salt filled his nose, and his cracked and calloused hands held the sheets firm.

The Spray crested over the waves, traveling downwind with great haste. Slocum locked the tiller in place and only held the sheets for posterity's sake, for The Spray was unparalleled in her ability to hold a steady course on her own. Slocum knew there ought to be naught but smooth sailing on this voyage, beginning his trip on the very same day the final hurricane of the season dissipated in the Sargasso Sea. Even still, his were a set of skills that brought him from the shores of Australia to the Southern Peninsula of South America with nary a map or proper chronometer, guiding himself with the moon and his memory alone, so he believed himself prepared for whatever the sea may send his way. No doubts or worries festered in Slocum's mind right until the ocean waters began to splash onto the deck.

Warm. The December waters of the Atlantic Ocean were warm. Slocum paused, and after cleating the sheets, he leaned over the starboard side and dipped his right hand into the flowing waters.

Warm, nearly scalding to the touch. Slocum grew weary. His

attempts to avoid hurricane weather seemed thwarted, but in all of Slocum's travels, he had never felt waters that ran so hot. These were not normal hurricane waters, but the thought of the storm they might be capable of brewing gnawed at his mind. He spoke to The Spray: "I know not what I've brought myself into, but all I need of you is the strength to bring me out." He left the sheets in their cleats, placing his trust in The Spray to hold course over his now shaken nerves. As the sun climbed higher, Slocum gazed above in terror as the blue morning sky began to curdle into an unnatural red haze.

His eyes narrowed, and as he saw the sky shift in hue before his very eyes, he spotted black clouds about the horizon. He whipped his head from East to West, and all around him, clouds the color of soot rolled in. It looked as though the heavens themselves were set ablaze, with black smoke from the combusting firmament encircling Slocum and his sloop. His doubt grew into denial, and he could only pray that his eyes betrayed what was truly before him. He took one last look at the sky and then brought his gaze toward the ocean ahead. He resolved that he should not alter course.

It was not long before the storm was upon Slocum. The rain pelted his round-brim hat, and he fought with the sheets to keep his boat steady. In all his years at sea, Slocum never learned to swim. Capsizing here, hundreds of miles from the shore would mean certain death. The Spray careened over billowed whitecaps, and the jet-black clouds had now blotted out the fiery red sky. To Slocum's eyes, this storm was far from the fiercest he had endured, but as the thunder rolled across the ocean, he could only pray his sloop would be spared by the coming lightning.

The warm waters soaked his clothes, which then became cooled by the brutal winds. His muscles tensed as he shifted his weight across the boat, dancing with the rocking of the sloop to keep her upright. The sun was swallowed up by the all-consuming clouds above, and the waters appeared before him as a churning mass of ink. Slocum gave all he had to keep The Spray steady, and in his mind, he prayed that she kept her proper course, but

116

as quickly as the storm descended, it began to rescind back into the sky.

The wind tapered off as the sails of The Spray grew limp. The clouds began to shrink back to whence they came, but this did not put Slocum's mind at ease, for the sky still burned red. The rays of the bloody sun beat down harshly upon the dead sea. By some means, Slocum could not fathom, the ocean had simply stopped. The waves and wind were completely abated, and The Spray drifted with dead sails across the mirror of the stagnant sea. With the sun at its meridian, it would be long before Slocum could gauge his location with the moon and his shattered clock, so he cleated the sheets and locked the tiller, committing to whatever direction The Spray had placed him in. Just as he began to sit down and regain his composure, he finally noticed the decrepit ship which had newly appeared along the horizon.

The ship was void of sail or sheet. It, too, was a sloop of similar design to The Spray, but even from afar, Slocum could see its rotting hull and crooked mast. Slocum never traveled with binoculars or any other optical instrument, so he squinted as best he could past the bow of his sloop to parse whatever details he could, all the while the sun reflected off the perfectly smooth waters. Slocum attempted to skull the boat, but the efforts this demanded were not matched by any results. All he could do was wait for the wind to return and watch as the derelict ship ahead grew larger and larger as some unseen force slowly brought the two sloops together. With no landmarks about him, and nary a cloud in the sky, Slocum was unable to determine whether he or the other ship was moving. He considered for a moment that perhaps the waters themselves articulated to ensure their meeting.

Slocum gazed at his clock. The chaos of the storm must have shattered its delicate mechanisms, as the hands were locked at high noon, never moving no matter how much time had elapsed. Slocum waited in this state of limbo while the sloop ahead drifted nearer.

To Slocum's mind, hours must have passed before the two sloops met, in spite of the sun never once moving from its apex.

As the ship approached, its disrepair came into full view. The rotting hull was pock-marked with small holes, and the stern of the boat was totally bereft of any tiller or rudder. The sloop slowly drifted to The Spray's starboard side, and in the cockpit of the derelict sat a man.

The man's bald head shone brightly under the sun, and the man appeared to be solely composed of skin and bones. His skin was tight on his yellow body as if he were nothing but a skeleton dipped in wax. He was naked save for a cloth which wrapped around his waist and under his crotch. Slocum initially thought him a corpse, but two bright eyes stared back at him, proving that this ascetic mummy still yet held life. Once their eyes met, a sickly grin spread across the man's face.

Slocum called out to him. "Who are you?" The man lifted his arm out and beckoned. His limbs appeared too thin to support their own weight, yet they still shifted and articulated. "I want not to shout to speak to you. Why don't you join me on my ship?" His arm slowly drifted back down to its resting position.

Slocum glared. "There isn't a chance I'm abandoning my ship. Why don't you come over here instead? Yours hasn't even any sails. If that storm were to come back, you'll be shattered long before you reach land."

The man snickered, his thin stomach undulating below his distended rib cage. "You're right. The storm will most certainly return, for we have only found itself within its eye. But I assure you that once it returns, your ship will fair no better than mine." He sucked a long, thin breath through his teeth. "I'm sure you've noticed by now that the weather movements we are experiencing are in no way natural. I'm sure you concluded whatever timepiece you have is broken, but they would be functional were they anywhere else but here. If you want to know why and wish to have even a snowball's chance in hell of survival, I implore you to join me, lest that sloop becomes thy coffin."

Slocum tensed, but he knew better than to show it. With great apprehension, he stood and walked toward the bow of his ship. He produced a long rope from under the deck, and he affixed it to the mast of The Spray. He grabbed the end of the rope and stepped onto the derelict, tying the rope to one of the cleats on the port side. After ensuring the cleat was fastened and that The Spray would not soon drift off with his absence, he sat across from the man, his gaze boring into the eyes of the peculiar being that should not have been able to draw breath.

The man took a long, deliberate gasp, and his voice came out croaking and dry. "I had thought I recognized you." His smile grew wrinkled and taut. He raised a thin bony finger toward his fellow passenger. "Joshua Slocum. I confess that I have yet to read your book, but I've been told much about you." The man lowered his hand. "I must thank you for accommodating my request. Considering my present state, this is about as loud as I can speak while maintaining my comfort. Yelling even as little as I did just then sapped me of much of my energy." The man's oily face maintained its genial grin, but Slocum hardened his stony visage.

"So, who might you be then? You look just about ready to give up the ghost. I find it hard to believe you survived that storm, what with your boat and body being as they are." "This ship, much like this body, holds far more strength than you might initially presume." A sharp snort shot through his nose as he smiled wryly. "But as I have noted, this coming storm will not discriminate between your ship or mine. Even a man of your considerable skill could not hope to forestall what's to come, whether you were to helm your trusty sloop or this rotting derelict."

A grumble escaped Slocum's lips. "You promised that I would be given some means of explanation regarding these…" He paused, betraying his fabricated air of confidence. "These puzzling developments. The sun has not abated for hours, and the sky runs red as blood. Where even are we?"

"The mighty Slocum, fessing to his ignorance." The man's delicate hands rapped together in a slow, hollow clap. "How very big of you. I will be direct. You and I have come here to die." If Slocum was fazed, he made sure it did not show. "You think that a suitable explanation?" The man shook his head. "Perhaps not, but that is about the long and short of it. Whether you remain in my boat or sail on with your own, you will never see land again."

"And for what reason should I abide by your judgment? I've seen storms far worse than what we just went through. Way I see it, there's no reason I can't suffer through the storm once we leave its eye."

The man sighed and shook his head once more. "Place your hand in the water Slocum." Slocum stared, but it seemed that the man would not continue until Slocum afforded him this indulgence. He leaned over the port side and felt the unmoving waters between the derelict and The Spray. They still ran hot to the touch.

"A man of your unmatched experience should know these waters belong well outside any domain of normalcy. Most any form of sea life would die in an ocean this warm, and yet where we find ourselves is the domain of a creature that thrives under these very conditions."

"Speak plainly, or I will cave in those jutting ribs of yours." Slocum's gaze grew harsh, and he began to tightly grasp his knees.

There was a pause as the man's eyes sparkled. He snickered and lifted his left arm, pointing his flat hand to the waters behind Slocum. The whirring sound of rope slack being pulled filled his ears, and he quickly turned about to find the pile of rope, the ends of which affixed The Spray to the derelict, rapidly disappearing over the port side. Slocum stood and watched as The Spray was pulled out towards the horizon, the rope almost fully taut. He dove to the port side cleat and wrapped his calloused hands about the rope, riding the tips of his feet against the side of the boat and pulling as much as his body would let him. His hands struggled to climb the rope, grasping and leaning to fight whatever force dragged the sloop away into that red expanse. With a great surge, the force wrested the rope from his grip with such strength that the rope burned his hands raw, and the cleat of the derelict popped off and was thrown out to sea. Slocum fell back and gazed in horror as his sloop was pulled away into the sea. Soon the ship slowed before whatever force which now controlled it held it stationary many yards away from the derelict.

From the ocean came five tentacles, grey tentacles the color of protoplasm, which spiraled up into the sky, far above the mast of The Spray. The base of the tentacles appeared wider than the tallest redwood tree, and the tips were thin as razor wire. The rubbery appendages jerked down, and soon Slocum's ship was wrapped in the embrace of a thousand suckers. Even from afar, Slocum clearly heard the creaks and groans of The Spray. It sounded like she was crying. In but a moment, the tentacles pulled tight, and the sloop was dashed into a thousand splinters. The tentacles receded into the warm ocean waters, and with it, The Spray sunk down into the sea.

It was some time before Slocum could bare to stand, still collapsed in the derelict next to the corpse of a man whose face was entirely relaxed in the face of the total destruction he had just witnessed.

The man broke the silence. "No matter how plain I speak, I believe any words I may render will do a disservice to what you have just witnessed." Slocum looked at the man, brought back to his senses by the bile-colored man sitting so close to him. He stood up and gazed one final time at the wreckage before turning back to the man.

"This explains nothing, you spurious wretch." He gave all he had to command some sliver of authority. "I have traveled across the entire face of this world. I have conquered every ocean. Never have I seen such an impossible creature. There is no conceivable way such a being could exist on this planet." He planted his feet and gazed defiantly at the man. "Explain how the thing exists without my knowing, or I shall drown you for letting my sloop be sunk and for playing so abhorrently with my senses."

A powerful cackle came from the man's throat. "You've no reason to doubt your senses. Your reaction, however, is entirely understandable. You seem to have mistakenly believed that it is possible for a man to 'conquer' the ocean, as you put it. Such a delusion is swiftly broken when faced with her true wonders."

The man pointed out to the sea. "This creature is of a size

that dwarfs any contraption of man. It burrows into the deep ocean floor to receive warmth which emanates from the center of the Earth. With a blowhole that crowns its slippery form, it pumps hot air into the surrounding waters. This accomplishes two things: the first is it allows the creature to swim out from its burrow and feast on the sea life, which dies when entering the water's warm thralls. The second is that it produces fierce, world-rending storms. The warmth of the water causes the surrounding air to rise, festering and swelling into the same sort of storm we find ourselves at the center of. It shall feast upon whatever it traps." The man glares at Slocum. "In the face of such power, how could one man in a wooden ship even begin to 'conquer' this vast universe below us?"

Slocum stewed in thought. "And for what reason should I believe your words?" The man snickered. "None. The outcome will remain the same. Soon enough, this ship shall be rendered into scrap, and we shall both return to the waters whence we came." The man's voice grew firm. "But know this: Heed not my words, and you shall die without truly understanding your fate."

Slocum sneered. "I know well my fate, and I have no fear of it. The bell tolls for all in due time. If now is when it tolls for me, then so be it."

The man's voice grew loud and raspy. His brow furrowed, and a scowl came over his face. "You understand nothing, Slocum. You don't merely die. Your essence returns unto the very waters you claim to have conquered. For before man, there was the land, and before land, there was the sea. For time unfathomable, the sea in her beauty grew and thrived, maturing into a world of which we primitive men can only perceive the surface. No matter what man builds or achieves, it will, in time, roll back to the ocean which gave him life. If Alexander's conquest ended with his empire's total destruction at the hands of the Greeks, what sort of conqueror would Alexander be? If you die, and all you have achieved is swallowed back up by that which you claim to have conquered, what sort of conqueror could you possibly be?"

Slocum scoffed. "So I am not a true conqueror, but I remain

to be so in the minds of men. My words and my children will carry on my legacy, and my accomplishments will be remembered for centuries after I pass."

The man once again sucked hard through his teeth, and his scowl contorted with scorn. "Men are foolish and fickle. Already your skills and abilities have been made meaningless by the workings of men. Men travel across the sea in primitive coal ships that force you and your ship into obsolescence. Your world and relevance are shrinking, Slocum. All you've done and all you've worked toward is being beaten out by the endless march of time. Soon too, will all the Vanderbilts and Cunards, which have rendered you and your sails irrelevant, be rended and replaced with increasingly convoluted contraptions. Man's endless drive toward progress holds none sacred, and all shall eventually do their part in fading from the memory of man."

Before Slocum was able to respond, the man continued. "But even as man evolves and harnesses ever more powerful sciences and technologies to ferry him across this planet, the oceans will prove to be far too vast of an expanse for him to ever truly fathom. Man can but skim across this swelling pandaemonium, and his role in this world is not to conquer it, for man is too small, too insignificant when faced with her mighty waters. Even you, Slocum, the only being whom man produced that could ever hold claim to the title of 'Conqueror of the Seas,' are further from conquering the waters than the burrowing termite is from conquering the ship, and in due time even you shall be returned to her embrace." The man catches his breath before concluding. "Soon will come the day when the last man speaks your name, and with him, all that you claim to have conquered will be wrested from what little influence you hoped to have possessed."

The man grimaced as he gasped for air, leaning his hands on his knees as his hollow chest sank and swelled. The black clouds began to roll in, and the wind slowly returned to the ocean, Whipping about the derelict ship. Looking at the man, Slocum merely laughed, and calm washed over his face.

"Thus is the nature of temporary beings. You are right. In

regards to this immortal sea, men cannot hope to claim any sort of lordship. It is the duty of every man born to eventually pass on, allowing for those who come after to replace all that he had known." The black clouds grew thicker and began to encircle the boat once more. The horizon soon became swallowed up, and the sky above grew black as the storm slowly approached the sun. "But where you seem to find despair in this duty, I find it rather reassuring. Already I and my accomplishments have been cheapened by the developments of man, and yet this does not negate what I have done. I, as a feeble, fleeting being, have wrested control of the natural, immortal world for but a single moment, with a family and a legacy that solely belongs to me." The winds grew strong and blew cold, and the sky was now smothered by the dark. "Eventually, this legacy will mean nothing, and my descendants will soon die out. But if I, as one of your so-called foolish beings, have left behind proof that I, Joshua Slocum, existed, be that proof fickle or fleeting, then I go gladly back into the waiting arms of the sea."

Below the sloop, the outline of a being began to rise toward the surface, growing ever nearer in the deep black waters. The man looked overboard, and he caught a glimpse of the terror which would soon devour the ship.

The man lept back. His head jittered, and the image of the abyss was burned deep into his moist eyes. Slocum, too gazed over the sloop, but he was not brought to madness by what he beheld. He looked at the man in pity. "You can talk all day about the inevitability of oblivion, but making peace with it is another matter altogether."

A shrieking howl escaped the man's dry lips. His body of skin and wax sprung to life, and he scrambled up the crooked mast of the derelict, screaming and gasping in horror. Slocum

looked up at the man and then brought his gaze toward the horizon. He stepped up onto the side of the sloop and, with arms outstretched in a welcoming embrace, cast himself into the sea. With a great rumbling, four tentacles spiraled up and around the derelict, and the man was brought back into the ocean again.

Verrill's account of St. Augustine's Monster
sourced from "Monsters of the Sea" (Richard Ellis, 1994)

Two Guitars

Alexander Kerr

The final chord of the song hung in the air, for a moment the only sound in the half-empty bar. As it died away, it was replaced with half-hearted applause from the bar's patrons. Hector smiled at them, inclining his head in polite acknowledgment. After a few seconds of applause, everyone turned back to their drinks and discussions.

Hector unslung his mahogany guitar, affectionately named Doc after the years of damage and repair it had been through, from his shoulders. He gently placed Doc back into a worn gig bag. Once a vibrant crimson, time faded the color to a dirty salmon. A full minute of struggling with the zipper passed before Hector managed to get the bag closed. He closed the notebook on the music stand and slipped it into a pocket on the outside of the guitar bag. He placed the stand and stool against the wall and stepped down from the bar's stage, a simple wooden platform half a foot high. As Hector weaved through the tables towards the bar, he smiled and nodded at the patrons, who made small efforts to return his greeting.

Upon reaching the bar, he pulled up a stool and sat, leaning the guitar bag against the lacquered wooden paneling. A bartender looked at him questioningly, but Hector waved the implicit request away. A few minutes passed, and Hector watched a TV in the corner aimlessly. A football game was on, but he didn't really know either team playing. At last, the manager stepped out from a backroom and grunted at the sight of Hector. Fishing into a back pocket, the manager withdrew a check and handed it to Hector, who then tucked it into his coat. "Thanks a lot. I'll see you again next week?"

"Afraid not. Nobody's been showing up for your shows."

"Are you serious? It's barely been a month."

"I'm really sorry, man, but you know business isn't exactly booming." He gestures behind Hector to vacant tables.

"I-" Hector trailed off, thinking of a retort.

"Look, Hector, it just doesn't make sense. The customers seemed to like that first song, but everything else bored them. Why don't you make a set list of covers? You may get a bit more traction that way."

"I don't want to do that. I want to play my own music."

"I understand, but you'll have to do it elsewhere. You're a good guy. I'm sure you'll bounce back."

Realizing arguing was just going to waste his time, Hector slid off the barstool and grabbed his guitar bag. A few of the tables closest to the bar gave him sideways glances as he strode to the door and opened it, probably more forcefully than he needed to. Hector stepped through and let the door shut behind him.

The walk home was short. He knew the next couple days would be stressful, trying to find a new source of income, but he'd known that would be the case when he chose to pursue music. At last, he rounded a corner to be confronted by the large neon sign "Blazing Night." Retrieving keys out of a coat pocket, Hector headed to a door in the alleyway, unlocked it, and ascended the cramped circular staircase, ducking his head to avoid a particularly low beam in the ceiling. After unlocking a second door, he unslung the bag from his shoulder, placed it into a corner, and threw his coat over the back of a chair.

Hector laid down on the cot, twisting to get comfortable amidst the mattress lumps. He stared at the popcorn ceiling and sighed while a faint throbbing from the club below began to filter through the floor. After a few moments, he turned on the stiff pillow, pushing his worries to the next day.

With a night of sleep on his side, Hector was much more optimistic. He'd never really liked playing at Leonard's—it was kinda grimy, and the customers weren't particularly friendly. He wasn't delusional, though. Making it in the music industry is hard, hours of thankless playing and practice, and plenty never see a penny for all their efforts. One step at a time is the way, starting with picking up some new gigs.

He got ready quickly, grabbed his guitar bag and coat, and was out the door. Hector walked two blocks to the nearest subway station. A cursory glance inside the station revealed a lack of authorities, so he hopped the turnstile and headed to the platform.

Hector disembarked at the central station. All around were performers vying for the attention of disinterested passengers. The train station was always bustling, but people were rarely in the mood for a performance. Instead, he walked a few blocks away. Wandering around a five-block radius from the station for a while rewarded him with a quiet but pretty well-trafficked corner. A few hours of playing resulted in a modest reward, $60-70 by the look of the guitar bag.

Packing up, Hector roamed the streets a while longer, stopping by a few cafes and bars advertising live music in their windows to request playtime. Altogether it wasn't a bad day. The money from busking would keep him fed for another week, and he had a few leads for recurring gigs.

He walked back to the central station. Inside, he stood contemplating the subway schedule and the grand clock mounted on the wall. The evening was still young, and there was a section of the city that he hadn't really explored yet. Joining a throng headed toward the platform, he jumped the turnstile farthest from the bored transportation authority. It was unlikely the woman was paying him any attention, but he'd rather not get fined and lose the afternoon's haul.

He got off at the penultimate stop on the line, emerging into an unfamiliar section of his home city. Unsure where to start, he followed the trickle of passengers from the subway stop, hoping to be led somewhere busier. He paid attention to his turns so he could retrace his steps, but otherwise just wandered. The streets were empty. It seemed to be an area sectioned for some revitalization in a few years but presently was mostly barren. No bustling street corners to perform on, one dingy bar that, when he entered, he received glares from every person present. Not a particularly welcoming area.

Deciding there was nothing to be gained, he turned down a street that he judged would head back toward the subway station. After a block, he passed a nearly empty storefront. Peeling letters above the window revealed it had once been "Orpheus Music Store." The walls were bare, peppered with holes indicating the store had once been covered floor-to-ceiling with shelves. The door was off its hinges and resting against an inside wall of the store. The windows needed a thorough wash, and exposed wires dangled from rusting light fixtures. Through smudges and old flyers, Hector could see some faded amateur graffiti against a back wall.

Sitting on a ledge inside was a well-worn guitar.

Blinking at it, Hector spun slowly to see if anyone was around to claim the instrument. The store had clearly been abandoned, and much of the street was in a similar state. Dissatisfied with the prospect of leaving a perfectly fine instrument to rot, he gently stepped across the threshold, broken glass crunching under his shoes. He picked up the guitar, inspecting it. He plucked an open string, but it didn't appear to be broken. In fact, the tone was rather good for having been sitting out for who knows how long. With Doc's bag slung over his shoulder and the new instrument in hand, he headed home.

"So we haven't ironed out the details exactly, but we're looking at one or two gigs a week and around $150 a gig. How does that sound?"

Two weeks of walking the streets, busking, and playing at open-mic nights had rewarded Hector with a new restaurant featuring live performances. He got lucky and was among the first musicians to volunteer to play. The recurring performances would provide a more steady income and be a new opportunity to perform his music. The general manager had requested a quick meeting before the restaurant's 4:00 pm opening time to go over some specifics.

"That sounds perfect. I'm so thrilled for the opportunity to be playing here." "Glad to hear it. Before I let you go, I should tell you about the scheduling. The first few weeks will be pretty random, but after that, we'll prioritize the most popular artists. It's just how the business works out."

"Okay, thanks for letting me know."

"Great, I can show you out." The pair stood and walked through the empty restaurant towards the door. Hector quickly assessed his repertoire; there were some clear frontrunners, but he realized he had no idea how much time needed to be filled.

"Oh, one more thing. About how long should the sets be?"

"Good question. Can't believe I forgot that. We're thinking between 40 and 50 minutes."

"Gotcha. I'll see you next week."

As the door closed behind Hector, he frowned and set off at a brisk walk. 40-50 minutes was doable, but the quality of the set concerned him. Usually, in public, he could repeat the same five songs as people came and went. Plus, most open mics didn't want anyone hogging the stage, so they limited pretty fiercely. To fill that set time, he'd have to play some of his older songs, which were pretty poor attempts at songwriting. The conclusion was obvious: write a couple new songs. It would be a busy week finishing the songs, practicing them, and performing them on the street, but the opportunity he'd been handed was not to be squandered.

Melodies and chord progressions were already forming in Hector's head as he ducked into the alley next to Blazing Night. After a moment fumbling with his keys, he bounded up the tight spiral staircase as quickly as he dared. He quickly opened and closed the apartment door behind him, dropped his coat over the back of a plastic chair, and dragged the chair toward his bed. He unzipped his bag, pulled out Doc, and sat on the bed, stretching his feet onto the chair.

He strummed a few chords and opened his notebook. He thumbed through the pencil-scratched pages until he came to one with some space and began writing lyrics as they came to him. Interspersed with the lyrics were some ideas for chords. The song was fairly simple, but he was determined to write something compelling, and so he sat scribbling for hours. Looking up through the apartment's small window, he could see the sun beginning its descent in the sky. Noise from tonight's band's sound check floated through the floors. Hector rolled his eyes, closed the notebook, and slipped into his bag's pocket. Shouldering the zipped bag, he opened the door, ready to find a quiet place to work, and cast his eyes back to make sure he hadn't forgotten anything. His eyes landed on the old guitar he'd rescued two weeks ago, which had so far lain dormant in a corner. He shrugged, grabbed the guitar, and headed to a public park nearby.

Hector passed through a stone arch entryway to the park. The cacophony of the bustling city faded away as he meandered through the nature. Not wishing to waste daylight, he identified a tree that looked comfortable enough and sat against it. He set the rescued guitar to one side, unpacked Doc, and retrieved the notebook from the guitar bag. Another half an hour of scratching out lyrics, reordering chords, and experimental strumming led to a draft he was happy with. Satisfied, he set Doc aside and picked up the new guitar.

Hector leaned back against the rough bark of the tree, the guitar resting comfortably on his knee. Hoping to brainstorm a few more ideas for a song before heading home, he strummed a chord at random. Instantly, his fingers began to fly across the fingerboard, shaping complicated chords and weaving together a beautiful melody. His eyes snapped open, and he let go of the guitar, pushing it onto the grass.

The guitar lay silent.

Hesitantly, Hector reached for it. He touched it gingerly, quickly withdrawing his hand. He picked it up again, settling it across his thigh. Closing his eyes once more, he began to play, and beautiful music poured from the guitar, unhindered by his amateur songwriting. Hoping to find some lyrics to go with the music, he opened his mouth to sing. It was as though the words were being pulled from him. His mouth shaped words and sentences which he had never written. It was as though the music had taken control of his body. The guitar and lyrics intertwined effortlessly, filling the surrounding area with harmony.

The music was happening without having to think. It was incredible. Unable to comprehend, Hector simply enjoyed listening to the music emanating through him. It could have been two minutes or twenty, but eventually, he stopped his fingers and closed his mouth, opening his eyes to a small crowd in a semi-circle around him. Seeing he had finished, they applauded gently but with great enthusiasm. Most of them continued on their way, but one woman approached him, asking, "That was fantastic. What's your name? Where can I find more of your music?"

Confused, Hector stammered out, "Th-thanks, my name is Hector. And uh, I have a few CDs from a while ago, but I doubt they'd be of much interest to you."

Shaking her head, she pointed at the guitar. "I'd be more than willing to pay for a recording of that."

Hector gazed around the dining room. Met with hushed conversations and expectant looks, he unzipped his bag. He placed his notebook open on a music stand and connected the guitar strap to Doc. Slinging it across his body, he settled onto a stool provided by the restaurant on the small performance stage. He plucked at the strings, tuning up for the performance. The muted conversations died away as the diners turned to face him, aware he would begin soon. He rechecked the tuning and his notes, preparing himself.

He began with his recent composition. It wasn't his best work, to be sure, but he was proud of the result of his time and effort. He had to concentrate intensely on his playing; the song had not yet been committed to his muscle memory. As he finished the second verse, poised to move to the final chorus, his concentration slipped. The result was a rather dissonant chord. Hector cringed but quickly moved on, hoping the listeners wouldn't take great notice. He recovered nicely, finishing the song strong. Yet, he couldn't help but kick himself over the slip-up.

Polite applause sounded through the restaurant. Looking out at his audience, none looked particularly impressed. Hector hoped to win them back with the next song, one of his favorites he'd written. He began to strum the guitar, the music and words flowing easily, the product of hundreds of performances. Without needing to concentrate much, he tried to gauge the diners' reactions to his music. Most were pretty neutral, but a few appeared to be dissatisfied. Hector refocused, trying to channel as much passion into the song as possible. He finished on a long note, ending breathless. The applause was noticeably milder than after the first song.

Hector frowned, considering. After a moment, he unslung Doc from his shoulder and placed it on the floor next to the stool. He retrieved the other guitar from where it was propped against a wall. An open strum revealed it to be in perfect tune.

Cautious, he began to play, and once more, the music started flowing unbidden. Heads that were beginning to lose interest turned back to him. Without any lyrics in mind, he swallowed hard and opened his mouth to sing. As it happened before, he did nothing, and the lyrics came to him as he sang them. The song materialized before him—he was merely the vessel for it. After a few minutes, he realized the song would have to end at some point, and as the thought came to him, the music began to transition to a conclusion, ending shortly thereafter. A stunned moment passed before the restaurant burst into applause, with a few of the customers cheering enthusiastically. Hector beamed back at them, giving a slight bow while seated on the stool, tears of joy and relief in his eyes.

Champagne glasses clinked.

"Attention, everyone, attention. I want to say something. The last few months have been a lot of work and stressful for us all, but after three top 20 singles, Hector's latest album has debuted at number nine on the charts. This is truly fantastic, especially for an artist so young in his career. Congrats, friend, and I look to many more years of partnership." From atop the desk, he pointed to Hector, raised his glass, and drank.

He stepped down from the desk as Hector walked towards him.

"Thank you for your kind words, Jared. It's been great working with you and everyone at the label, but I really think the focus should be on the music rather than me."

"Bah, you're too modest, you know that?" He threw an arm around Hector's shoulders. "C'mon, let's go celebrate."

Hector mingled at the launch party, accepting congratulations and making small talk. He knew a few of the executives and producers after having worked with the record label for his past albums, but many of the faces were unfamiliar to him. Altogether though, he was not having a great time. Apparently, it was clear. Friends and strangers expressed concern, asking if Hector was feeling well. He waved it away, claiming to have slept poorly. Promotional material with his face plastered across it stared down at him from the walls, causing great discomfort.

Eventually, Hector realized he wasn't throwing the party and could leave if he wanted to. Most of the people there were just using the event as an excuse to socialize or drink during the day. Not many people seemed particularly concerned with him. Excusing himself from the group he was in, he navigated through the crowd to Jared. Hector thanked him for the event, but feigned fatigue, explaining that he was going to leave early. Jared made a vague attempt to convince him to stay but didn't try too hard.

Hector retrieved keys out of his pocket and unlocked his car as he exited the label's office. He drove 15 minutes back to his house, a significant upgrade from the small apartment above Blazing Night.

After arriving home, he dropped his coat over the back of an armchair before collapsing onto a sofa in the living room. He let out a long sigh, rubbed his face, and tousled his hair. The room was strewn with various recording implements. Amps were stacked in a corner, cables crisscrossed the floor, a keyboard stood in front of an ottoman, on which rested Doc, and on a stand in the corner was the guitar he had rescued. He stared at the guitar, considering it. Abruptly, he stood back up, carefully navigating his way across the floor. Hector grabbed the guitar from its stand and stared intently at it. After the first restaurant show he had performed with it, he spent almost two months trying to figure out how it made such music. In the end, he gave up, simply accepted it, and rode its ability to his current stardom.

Spinning on his heels, Hector traversed the room again but passed by the couch, ascending a staircase to the home's upper level. In the hallway between the master and guest bedrooms, Hector gently leaned the guitar against a wall. He pulled down the ladder to his home's attic and climbed up. Since moving in, the attic had remained untouched, mainly being used for long-term storage space. Shuffling a few boxes around, he cleared a space atop some taped-up containers. Descending the ladder again, he grabbed the guitar leaning against the wall before climbing back up into the attic. He placed the guitar on the space he'd cleared, turned back around but hesitated. Most would kill to be in his position. Hector was signed to a record and was releasing successful music, but he was unable to enjoy the spotlight any longer. He wanted his music to be his own. He left the attic and pushed the ladder back into place.

"I think I know what I want to do for my next album, and I wanna shake things up a little bit."

Jared's eyes narrowed slightly, and he gestured at the chair in front of his desk. "Let's not be drastic, Hector. The first albums were fantastic. I don't think now's the time to be 'shaking things up.' Do you know what I mean?"

Taking a seat, Hector responded. "I do, but I'm afraid I'm gonna have to insist on this; it's extremely important for me."

Jared exhaled slowly, spinning slightly in his chair. His eyes wandered above Hector's head, gazing at the gold and platinum records that adorned his wall. Suddenly his eyes snapped back to Hector's. "Well, as long as you maintain the same appeal of the first few, I suppose it will be fine. What kind of new sound did you have in mind?"

"Well...I'm not quite sure yet."

Brow furrowing, Jared asked, "I thought you said you knew

what you wanted to do?" "Yes, I did. I don't know what it will sound like, but it's going to be a solo album." A smile spread across Jared's face but didn't reach his eyes. "I thought all your albums were solo."

"Oh well, in a sense, they've been solo, but this one is truly going to be just me." "Well, it doesn't seem as though you're going to be swayed." Jared stood up, stepped around his desk, and opened the door. "Let me know when you're ready to record." "Oh, I will," said Hector as he exited the office.

Hector turned to close the office door, nervous at the prospect of writing an album without the guitar's help, and just before the door swung shut, he could hear a sigh from the office, accompanied by an exasperated mutter of "artists."

Progress on the album was slow. Hector wrote with intricate purpose, rewriting lyrics dozens of times, recording take after take to make the perfect songs. Without the flawless improvisation granted by the guitar, his pace slowed considerably, but at least all the music was truly his.

"Usually, his improvisation is near perfect; honestly, I don't know how he does it. It usually takes five attempts at most for an album-worthy recording. The angst and indecision here is a little worrying. He's been writing for so long. It's unlike him." The producer behind the soundboard glanced at Jared. "Have you heard the demo for the new single?" "I have not."

The producer grimaced and gestured to a pair of headphones on the desk. "You may want to take a listen."

Frowning, Jared picked up the headphones, settled them over his ears, and widened his eyes at the producer, indicating he should play the demo. As the song progressed, Jared's face cycled through confusion, concern, and, finally, anger.

"Can you get him out of the booth?"

"Right away." The producer thumbed a button, "Hey Hector, Jared wants a quick chat." Hector signaled a thumbs up, removed his own headphones, set Doc on its stand, and walked to the studio's door. The door had scarcely closed behind him before being barraged by Jared.

"What's going on? Is this a joke?"

"Is what a joke?"

"The demo," Jared answered, gesturing towards the discarded headphones behind him. "Oh, you don't like it?"

"No, I don't like it!"

"Well, what's wrong with it?"

"What's wrong with it? It feels cheap, amateur." He sputters for a second trying to vocalize his frustration. "It's just bad."

Frowning, Hector went quiet for a moment, contemplating. Then he shrugged and responded, "This is where I am creatively. I know it's different from my previous stuff, but it's important to me. This is authentic."

"Authentic? I can't pay my staff with authenticity!"

"I understand, but just give me a chance."

Jared closed his eyes, took a deep breath, and opened them again. "You have one chance, and that is only because I promised you could do this. Plus, the paperwork has already gone through. But I want you to know I am not thrilled with the state of that demo. I very much hope that it is not representative of the album."

"Thanks for the feedback. I can make some improvements."

The album did not do well.

On release day, Hector spent hours on the couch, reading reviews and comments online. Around midday, he had finished watching a fourth reaction video and got up to make himself some lunch when the phone rang. He slipped an earpiece into his ear and set his phone on the counter. He listened as various executives commented on the performance of the album. He finished making a light lunch and sat back down before hanging up that call. Ten minutes passed before he picked up another from Jared, who was a little stressed out by the day's course since he had vouched for Hector. This led to an uncomfortable conversation culminating in a frustrated "Cut the crap, or we'll have to part ways." Hector had mostly shrugged off the earful from the label, but what cut deep was the criticism from the public. Scathing reviews hailed the album as 'immature songwriting,' 'a barely competent display of lyricism and instrumental skill,' and 'shallow melodies and messages that fail to live up to their album's predecessors.' Hector wanted his music to inspire and spread happiness, but instead, it did the opposite. The most lenient of comments cited potential, some embers that could be fanned into a flame given training and practice. Of course, these were accompanied with the obligatory comments about the album being worse than the previous ones.

Hector had truly dug deep while writing the album, and he could tell he was improving while writing it. Even on days where creativity was slow, he made sure to practice for two hours at least. But despite all that, the progress was too slow. Even though his skills improved, he could tell they weren't good enough to win back an audience. He was tempted to walk away from the

label altogether and pursue his passion on his terms. However, a part of him felt guilty at the thought of rejecting the guitar when it had provided a path to success, albeit not the one Hector had envisioned.

Excerpts from reviews echoed around Hector's head, mixing with various personal thoughts about whether to embrace the guitar. A pounding headache began brewing. Standing up from the couch, he navigated through the mess of instruments and furniture. He grabbed his keys off a hook next to the front door, stopped only to pat his pockets to ensure he had his wallet, and left the house. Too preoccupied to pay attention to where he was walking, Hector found himself outside the subway station. On a whim, he boarded a train towards the city center. He decided he could visit the park, and maybe it would help clear his head. The ride was a blur, and when he stepped off the train, he automatically headed toward the park. The city on a Friday night was starting to come alive, but Hector passed by crowded bars and restaurants without a second glance. The roar of the city was reduced to white noise as he processed. Passing into the park, he wandered through, finally sitting against a tree.

He let his eyes wander, and in the distance, he could see the tree where he had sat and played the guitar. It seemed like a lifetime ago. He reflected on everything that had happened, all within sight of where his life had changed. Then all of a sudden, something clicked. Hector fished his cell phone out of his pocket and dialed Jared, who picked up the phone before the first ring finished.

"Have you decided already?" Jared asked, somewhat confused.

"I have," Hector replied.

Marigolds In May

Chloe Counts

Tonight was the town hall's most important night of the year, the Debutante Ball. Outside, it was a clear May night in Ambrose. There were few cars on the road, and the large, elegant houses of the local neighborhood sat in silence, maids and butlers keeping warm in their quarters while the residents were off celebrating beneath the sharp spotlight of society. Tonight, they gathered in the jewel of the village: the town hall ballroom.

It looked like the ballroom had been coated with a fresh layer of snow. The ceiling was bright and dome-shaped, with a crystal chandelier hanging at its center. Light refracted around the room like snowflakes falling delicately onto the dozen white-clothed tables. Grand centerpieces of white roses adorned each table, and seated there were girls in their late teens with crimped curls and satin white dresses. At my table, there was a small basket of floury bread that the girl to my right was nearly inhaling. Marissa, I thought. We had been neighbors my whole life, and I'd watched her grow up with less supervision than myself. I wanted to kick her under the table, but I remembered my mother telling me you couldn't teach things like sense.

If this were a snowy scene, then I'd call the priest's greeting the first footprint. He cleared mucus from his throat and into the microphone at the front of the room. We all snapped our attention to him with the blank stares of deer in headlights. I say we because I found my reflection in the shine of the flower vase. I looked just as dumbfounded as the rest of the girls, though I guess I was.

"Welcome," the priest gruffed. "To the annual Debutante Ball." The priest looked taller than usual. I smiled when I noticed the small silver stool his long robe revealed when he lifted

his arms. The priest was a small and mouselike man, which it seemed didn't fall in line with the image they were going for tonight.

The priest continued with a speech that I had heard many times. I had been attending the grand event as long as I could remember. Today, however, was my first and only as a debutante myself. While the priest droned on, I felt my heart rate quicken and my dress itch terribly. I shifted my glance to the crowd surrounding the outer edge of the ballroom. There, in a pale yellow dress, I spotted my mother. She looked like she was trying to hold back tears until she caught my eye, which made her flash an unnatural smile and nod in my direction.

As the priest neared the end of his speech, it felt like all the air had been sucked out of the room. Everyone was holding their breath, waiting to hear who would be chosen this year. I thought back to my younger sister Emma who was at home, probably cuddled up on the couch with a novel of some kind. Emma would never be a debutante as she had broken her nose a few years back, causing it to become grossly crooked in a way that would surely offend the high society of Ambrose.

I could hear Emma laughing in my ear like she did when we went about our usual under-the-table debutante gambling. Each year one debutante was chosen to make the ultimate sacrifice in some sort of ritualistic attempt to keep us girls grateful, or rather, keep us in line. They claimed the selection to be random, but the trend of misbehaved girls over the years spoke otherwise. Emma had bet on me this time around, not because she thought I'd be chosen, but in a last-ditch effort to allow her to "accidentally" break my nose. I had bet on Marissa to remind her I would be just fine.

I quickly blinked out of my thoughts as soon as I heard the priest beginning the last few lines of his speech and pull from his engulfing robes a knife. The blade's ruby-encrusted handle radiated importance in the large room so devoid of color. I smiled and, for a moment, thought of what it might feel like to be cut by such a talisman. It would be an honor, but would it hurt? Of course, it would, I thought. I winced and glanced over at Marissa. Her thoughts didn't seem to range so far. With the glazed, wide eyes of a child, Marissa looked at the knife like it was a shiny new toy, something a toddler would squeal over. It made my stomach turn.

The priest held the knife over his head and closed his eyes. Time stood still as we waited to hear who it would be.

"Marissa,"

She gasped, and her eyes welled with tears. I heard her mother cheer, and people begin to clap. Take that, Emma, I thought. But as Marissa stood and moved forward, I saw her feet wobble in her heels, and my satisfaction faded. I thought of the lessons my mom had given me to make sure I walked better than that. I wondered if things would be different if Marissa had gotten lessons too.

When she reached the front of the room, I couldn't look and instead settled my gaze at the trembling hands in my lap. The itching of my dress became so intense I couldn't help but reach up and itch my shoulder. I knew there would be pink scratches on my skin, but it seemed silly to worry about pink when I knew what was coming.

You would think there would be grief or anger to break the silence, but the room remained still as Marissa took the knife and performed the ritual. She could have screamed or resisted, I suppose, but there wasn't really a point, and I don't think such an option even so much as crossed her mind. By the time I blinked open my eyes, Marissa's dress was no longer white, and I felt an unfamiliar feeling wash over me. Her face looked as though it were made of porcelain, and her eyes were lifeless and glazed over like a doll's.

I hadn't noticed how pretty she was until that moment.

Her body was lying on the floor in front of the priest's post. He hopped off his stool, and one of his feet landed on her face, squishing it and leaving an imprint of his shoe. He then announced the next portion of the evening: the dance. I had learned ballroom dancing as a child and was accustomed to the steps. All my practice, however, was done with my younger sister, Emma, whose mistakes and shimmering laugh made it enjoyable and easy. The stakes were higher tonight, though, and I knew my enjoyment was not on the list of this evening's priorities.

A small, chubby woman sat at the piano and began to play a simple, lilting fox trot. I missed Emma dearly. At this point in the evening, the men in attendance would choose a debutante to dance with – a sign of respect and a step towards the ultimate goal of the evening: to find a wife. Around me, the tables had been cleared, and all the debutantes, me included, stood and waited to be chosen. Some girls looked confident with sly smiles and posture that accentuated their figures; their hips tilted to one side as they eyed each potential suitor with cat-like prowess. Others held their arms around their chests and stared at the ground. I was in the latter category, shifting awkwardly and pretending to be fascinated with the silver bracelet that adorned my wrist.

When I finally dared to take in the scene around me, an older man was striding in my direction. I reached up and itched the collar of my dress again, and gulped. Mr. Rothenburg must have been in his mid-fifties. He was tall with dark, oily hair and had a hungry look about him, like if I stepped too close, he might just bend down and take a bite. I knew this was meant as a compliment. I was the first girl chosen and by one of the wealthiest, highest-class men. Though, I also knew Mr. Rothenburg had been looking at me with that craving look ever since my childlike body started to mature. He must have been ecstatic to see me as a debutante – finally old enough to be thought of and touched in that way.

His hands explored my waist, and I felt his nails dig into my hips, causing my eyes to water. I wished he would draw blood so I could ask him to stop, but it seemed he knew what he was doing. I caught his wife's eye from the balcony. She was a silent, gentle-tempered woman, but I could see a cruel jealousy fizzle under her smile. She had been a debutante herself a few years ago. My dress started to itch again.

I pushed these thoughts and the itching of my dress out of my head and tried to flash the smile I had practiced at Mr. Rothenburg. It must have come out too enthusiastic because he took it as a sign to pull me closer. He smelled like fish oil, a thick scent that gathered in the back of my throat and made me gag.

I desperately looked away and again and took a second to notice the rest of the girls. Some had been chosen by older men as well. They all appeared to carry their discomfort better than I did. Others had been chosen by the boys of our town that were in search of a wife. They held their debutantes with looks like children on Christmas morning. I wanted a husband, or more so, I needed a husband. I knew Mr. Rothenburg dancing with me was a step in the right direction, signaling to the other families I was worthy of such attention. But in this moment, this most pragmatic and traditional practice felt painfully worthless compared to its cost. Mr. Rothenburg pressed his thin lips to my ear.

"Are you having a nice evening?" he growled, his hot breath collecting in my ear. "Yes," I choked. "It's been lovely."

He chuckled and asked me if I wanted to take a walk.

"I've been looking forward to dancing," I said. "Why don't we take a walk later?"

Clearly frustrated, he said, "Of course, whatever you want, doll." Over his shoulder, I noticed Marissa, and my contempt for her sloppy manners waned further. I both envied her and felt for her an inconsolable ache in the pit of my stomach.

The dance continued, and I was passed around from Mr. Rothenburg to several boys. Two of them shorter than me, and all of them even touchier than Mr. Rothenburg. By the end, I felt desensitized to Frankie Bellingham's hand slipping down my lower back further than was proper. The dancing continued until it was time for more speeches and drinks. I felt numb. The only thing that kept me attached to my material presence was the itching of my dress. It burned and crawled up my neck and down my windpipe, which began to constrict in response. I excused myself to the lady's room and, instead, snuck out to the garden.

It was a cool May evening. My whole body relaxed when the fresh air hit my face. The garden was filled with flowers of all colors. The first to catch my attention were a patch of golden and orange marigolds. It was dark out, but small lanterns lining the pathway illuminated the flowers and made them glow. Emma loved marigolds, so I picked one and stuffed it in the hem of my gown. The dress still itched, but the flower reminded me the night was almost over.

I sat on the bench at the side of the path and closed my eyes, meditating on this anticlimactic experience. It was every little girl in Ambrose's dream to be in my position, yet being celebrated and lusted over felt more bitter than I had anticipated. I opened my eyes and looked down at my dress. I resented my chest that peaked out of the neckline. I resented my waist and hips and every piece of me that gave these men the right to -

Crunch. I snapped my attention up, and there was Mr. Rothenburg stepping on a twig and approaching me.

It was like he was a spider, and I was a fly caught in his web.

"Finally," he said, "our walk."

"Oh, I was just heading back in." I knew this wouldn't please him, but the frustration I was sitting in gave me somewhat of a reckless confidence. My dress itched terribly, and I squirmed beneath it as Mr. Rothenburg took a step closer. I gently shifted further away on the bench, and the flower fell out of my dress. Without thinking, I reached down to pick it up. Mr. Rothenburg lunged forward, sending me flying off the bench and onto the plot of marigolds. Before I could sit up, I felt his weight knock the wind out of me as he took position.

I saw what happened next as a third-party viewer, as if in a dream, watching the horrible scene from a window in the sky. The girl wore a twisted expression of rage as he tore her dress and reached between her legs. She struggled and reached for the nearest lantern. It burned her fingers, but she held on anyway and threw it as the oily-haired head now approaching her lap. The part of her dress he had torn off went up in flames and engulfed him entirely. The flames licked her legs, but she managed to pull them out before they consumed her too.

I soon returned to my body and watched his ugly face melt like it was made of wax. The marigolds caught fire beneath him and glowed even brighter than they had before.

I drifted back over to the stone bench and sat, my eyes still glued to the horror that was unfolding in front of me. Most of Mr. Rothenburg was gone now, and what I had done slowly began to settle in. He deserved it, I told myself. He hurt me. But this wasn't the kind of town where that kind of logic rang true.

I sat on that bench for a long time until all that was left of the fire and Mr. Rothenburg was ash and ember. Until the chill of the evening crawled under my skin and caused goose bumps to rise. Until the ball let out, and the haughty residents of Ambrose flooded the garden and began their drunken strolls home. I kept my eyes on where the marigold patch had been and placed the one I had picked in my hair. My mother finally found me towards the end of the procession and immediately began questioning me. Where had I gone? What could I have been doing that was more important? What on earth had happened to my dress? With my eyes still on the thing tendrils of smoke rising from the marigold plot, I told her I left for some fresh air and tripped, ripping my dress, and was too embarrassed to go back in.

She put her arm around me, and our gazes intertwined as we both watched the last few embers sputter to life and drift back to the ground. "Did someone hurt you?" she said.

I was silent. It didn't matter. He couldn't hurt me anymore.

"It's going to be ok," she whispered. Her voice wavered, and I heard her sniffle. I had done something terrible, but here in my mother's arms, it didn't matter. "I'm glad you got out of there when you did," she chuckled. "I swear the priest rambled longer than I'd ever heard this year."

She looked at me and stroked my cheek, and soon we got to witness Marissa's departure from the town hall. The staff of the building were dressed in formal white suits and carried her body on a wooden stretcher past us. One of the staff members briefly tripped, and the jostle caused Marissa's arm to unbend from her chest and flop over the side of the stretcher. I watched her delicate hand dangle, and they continued on.

"Wait," I said. They didn't stop, but the lady that had tripped turned her head to look at me. It was a pitiful and condescending stare that made me feel that itching up my neck again, but before I looked away, I noticed the marigold tucked behind her ear.

We walked home shortly after, and when I finally made it to my queen bed, I couldn't relax. The scene played again and again in my mind. I tossed and turned and prayed and eventually gave up and let myself cry. The marigold was on my nightstand, staring at me with its bright pedals and laughing at me with its fiery, golden sheen.

I sat up and grabbed it, tucking it into the drawer of my nightstand. I thought of how long it would take for it to dry out and die. I wished the process would go faster.

With the flower out of sight and the Debutante Ball done with, I turned over and finally found sleep.

Marda's Moon

Casey Bloome

It was windy in the skies above Marda. Wind was a constant part of life, but Corey had chosen this particular time because of the unusually high wind speeds. Marda's largest moon, Asda, was reaching its perigee, coming closer to Marda than it would for many months. The atmospheres of the binary planets were mixing, creating regions of interference that resulted in a jumble of air pressures. This created unpredictable winds and combined the precipitation with the churning ocean below, resulting in the wildest rainstorms imaginable. This extreme weather would render Corey's exact position undetectable by radar. That gave her a head start.

Corey shot through the air, body tilted forward, her feet slightly lower than her head, with limbs extended as far as she could muster. This was basic windsuiting: limbs out meant more surface area for the flaps between her arms and legs, which meant more lift from the wind. Corey had seen footage of flying squirrels mid-flight from archival footage brought over from Earth after humanity expanded to this star system millennia ago. A person in a windsuit looked like a flying squirrel: thin membranes connected her outstretched limbs as the wind billowed and propelled her forwards. Windsuits were based on the Earth wingsuits of old: the biggest changes were the incorporation of electric heating and communication equipment and the conspicuous red Dree Inc. logo on the back.

Dree would call what she was doing theft. And legally, that was accurate; Corey didn't own this windsuit, though she'd certainly earned it after her years of repairing turbines for Dree. Dree owned nearly everything on Marda, and others could only use it with the company's permission. Corey certainly didn't have permission for taking the windsuit, let alone the data drive. What she was doing wasn't wrong, anyway, just illegal.

By now, employees at Dree would have already noticed the windsuit missing and would be tracking Corey's position as best they could through the rain. She expected that right now, there would be three or four Dree windsuiters chasing her, but they wouldn't catch up while Corey was still flying. She'd spent her whole career flying around Marda, and she knew the skies better than any of them. Nobody could catch an updraft, survive a turbulent day, or weave through the white stalks of wind turbines like Corey. She used to imagine herself like the owls or eagles of old, swooping through trees and vegetation in pursuit of prey. But now she was the one being pursued, she was the prey. Oh well. She'd only ever seen a bird once, anyway. It had been in a cage.

Rain pelted every square inch of Corey's windsuit—even the bottom, as updrafts carried droplets from every direction. Thankfully, the suit protected her from the worst of the harsh weather; the hydrophobic polymer prevented the water from soaking in, while the thin insulation kept her warm enough to prevent her from freezing to death. Her goggles were another matter: raindrops stuck on the visor, obscuring her view. Normally, this wouldn't be a problem. They hardly ever flew windsuits in the rain, and when they did, they used the electric heaters in their suits to prevent the water from pooling. But right now, Corey had her suit's electronics turned off. Powered off, she was disconnected from Dree's system, so they couldn't take control of her suit. Otherwise, they could lock its joints in place or even take control remotely, so that Corey would be trapped in a windsuit piloted by someone miles away. Even though the rain would interfere with the connection, she still couldn't take that risk.

Now she had a choice: she could try to use one gloved hand to wipe her mask mid-flight, but she'd have to be quick because any movement would upset her aerodynamics and throw her slightly off course. The other option was to let water build-up, but pretty soon she'd be flying blind, into an area with a lot of turbines.

A white spire flashed past her. She was entering the windiest corridor, also the place where the most turbines stood. She couldn't risk crashing into one face-first. She flinched at the thought. Corey reached up with her right hand, quickly swiped water off her visor, and returned to her flying pose. She tilted over during the effort but righted herself easily. She exhaled with relief and caught another updraft, gaining lift. She was overthinking things, but really, she was doing fine. She might even make it out.

Over the next few hours, the wind and rain picked up, but Corey felt lighter and lighter. This wasn't just relief at not seeing any Dree agents: she was also becoming physically lighter, as she was close enough to the transiting moon now to be feeling its gravitational pull. But she was aching like a marathon runner. Windsuiting didn't require great strength or agility, but holding the same gliding position for hours was excruciating. Her muscles had been tensed the whole time, and it didn't help that she was fearful of being chased and caught. She needed to stop for the night. Technically it was still daytime, but Asda above was in the process of an hours-long stellar eclipse, and Corey and these turbines were in the path of totality, blanketed by darkness. Still, she was exhausted. Time to find somewhere to rest.

She allowed herself to relax, losing altitude and speed as she glided towards a turbine, its base, and stalk lit by convenient white lights, beacons in the dark. Her controlled descent ended at its circular base, and she was careful not to be splashed by the waves careening over the side. As if it would make a difference— she was already soaked. She angled herself upright, and her feet touched down.

Immediately, she collapsed against the cold metal. Her heart was pounding and her breaths were ragged. She felt her zipped pocket to make sure the data drive was still inside. With relief, she sagged down against the frame, fully prepared to fall asleep right there, but a rude wave splashed over the side of the turbine's base, drenching her and reminding her that she wasn't yet safe.

She crawled to the back of the turbine. She found the rungs of the ladder and began climbing. The ladder shook slightly, producing tremors that she felt through the cold metal bars. Corey was careful not to get her windsuit caught in the cage that enclosed the ladder, meant to catch any windsuiter unfortunate or inexperienced enough to be so buffeted by the wind that made its way around the turbine to lose their grip on the ladder. But this cage was rarely used, as this turbine was several knots away from the Dree compound, and as such, were serviced only by expert windsuiters such as Corey. Still, better safe than sorry.

Exhausted, images of the past creeped into Corey's head as she recalled when she and her friends would race to climb the outside of the ladder cage. The slats of the cage were vertical, so it was tricky, but done correctly, one could scramble up the outside faster than the inside. Done incorrectly, a climber would lose their grip and be swept away by the wind, and, barring an updraft or sufficient maneuvering skill, they would tumble through the air for a few moments before splashing down into the ocean below, unharmed but embarrassed.

Corey ascended rung by rung and heave by heave, spurred on by the thought of the rest she would find at the top. At least some of the rain was blocked by the thick stalk of the turbine, while the wind curled around the sides lazily, as if finally experiencing calm after hours of gales.

Corey reached the flat section at the top. From here the rungs were slanted forward, angled towards the wind. The protection from the wind that Corey had enjoyed by being behind the turbine was suddenly gone. Up ahead, the door to the maintenance compartment stood, which would afford Corey some temporary shelter from the wind. Straining, she put hand over hand as she crawled forward, keeping her body close to the metal. She could feel the wind slipping under her chest, threatening to lift her into the air. Then, the wind dropped as Corey fell into the shadow of the compartment.

She fumbled with the latch with her gloved hands, steadying

herself by holding her feet under the last rung of the ladder. Finally, the door opened and she stepped inside. She took a carabiner from the wall, zipped it out, and clipped it to her suit. She slid inside and pulled the door shut behind her. She was barely able to take her mask off and turn the turbine's heater on before exhaustion overcame her and she fell asleep.

The thrum of electricity woke her up. Corey sat up fast, eyes wide open. The turbines deactivated themselves for most of the duration of Asda's perigee: the extreme winds meant that they could spin too fast and overclock, possibly even rip themselves apart. If the turbines had turned back on, that meant that the wind speed had decreased, which meant that Asda would be leaving soon—

She pushed open the door. The rain had stopped, and the air was filled with clouds. She breathed a sigh of relief as she saw the colossal Asda still looming overhead. The massive blades of the turbine whipped around behind her. She still had a few hours to make it, but she had to leave now.

Corey stretched for a minute, waking up the arm she had slept on while psyching herself up. She was thankful that before sleeping she used the reserve electricity in the turbine to dry herself with the heater: she could have gotten hypothermia. But now it was a nice morning, with a smattering of clouds occasionally parting to reveal the moon looming above. The sunlight shot sideways, in the narrow space on the horizon between Asda and Marda, casting long shadows. The weather made her optimistic. She tried to ignore the soreness in her limbs.

Corey gave one last look at the turbine she used to service, appreciating its elegant curves and shining metal. These swooshing blades helped generate the entire planet's electricity, assisting the livelihood of everyone on Marda. She was loath to leave, but she had to, in order to do justice to Dree. Anyway, she wouldn't be able to live with herself if she didn't try. She felt her pocket again for the minuscule drive, put on her visor, and jumped.

She soared through the air towards the catenoid between Marda and Asda, where the ocean bulged upwards as it was pulled towards the moon's gravity. This was going well! She hadn't seen any signs of Dree. Perhaps they didn't notice the windsuit and the drive missing or didn't count them as valuable enough to waste resources on. Asda hung in the sky, and round its perimeter, Corey could see the lights of civilization. The government of Asda worked hard on maintaining the delicate balance between the binary planets, ensuring that the elliptical orbit remained stable. Over the millennia, most of Asda's oceans had drained onto Marda, pulled in by the gravitational giant. Now what remained on Asda were the ridges and valleys that used to be undersea mountains obscured by oceans. Mountains that wind had trouble flowing through, which meant no wind turbines, which meant no Dree Inc. And for Corey, that meant freedom.

It was a nice day despite the earlier rain, and in the air hung clouds with the most random assortment of shapes possible, the result of the mixing atmospheres of Asda and Marda. The skyline was beautiful, with the white of the turbines and clouds dotting the vista of the blue skies and the bluer ocean below, not to mention the massive gray moon above. Then something red crept into view, in between Corey and the atmospheric catenoid connecting Marda and Asda. She recognized it instantly: it was the Battery Barge.

About once a month, a Dree shipping barge would come across the ocean, loaded with a giant empty battery. They'd hook it up to the turbines, and then take all the electricity generated back to the Dree compound. Corey had once been offered a job on the barge, and a high-paying one at that, but she'd decided to stick with windsuiting. She loved the skies and didn't want to be confined to the surface of a sphere. Plus, the barge was too well supervised for her to execute her plan.

But what was the barge doing here? The batteries in the turbines had been emptied just a few days ago; Dree was wasting energy by sending it out again. Then Corey realized: they were sending it after her! She was a high priority to them after all. Dree, to whom nothing was more important than the bottom line, deemed Corey a big enough threat to send their largest ship and its crew after her. But that didn't scare her. In an odd way, she felt honored.

But the barge was right under the Marda-Asda catenoid. It was a blockade: she'd have to practically fly above the barge to make it in time. She gritted her teeth and leaned forward, as the wind ruffled her hair. She eyed the huge white cloud connecting Marda and Asda, surrounded by a few grey specks: terrain, possibly, ripped from Asda thanks to Marda's overwhelming gravity.

As she got closer, she saw blue drones flying above the barge. No, these were people, wearing the blue windsuits of Dree. Clever, to choose a color that Corey wasn't wearing, so she couldn't blend in. Seeing how badly she was outnumbered, she reconsidered her earlier thought about being scared.

She flew low to the ocean, hiding from the barge and the windsuiters as best as she could, but it was useless in her red windsuit. Dree chose that color for the windsuits on purpose, Corey knew. They said it was so that windsuiters could be found in emergencies or if they needed rescuing, but the real reason was that windsuiters could be spotted easily if they attempted escape. Well, it worked.

"Miss Olis, approach the Battery Barge at once."

The commanding voice, amplified through the loudspeakers on the side of the ship, carried over the ocean despite the roar of the wind. Corey ignored it. She'd be past it in a minute. "Miss Olis, you are in possession of stolen company property. Return to the barge immediately or we will be forced to incapacitate you."

Corey swerved towards the barge as if to obey, but then turned back again. Maybe the momentary confusion would buy her time.

Nope. "Miss Olis, we will now attack you," the voice said calmly. "Don't say we didn't warn you."

Then the flock of blue windsuiters descended. They split into two groups: One seemed to be tailing her, while the other came towards her, head-on. Two suiters came at Corey from above. She saw them in her peripheral vision and dodged just in time. Something nylon green fell into the ocean behind her: they'd tried to drop a net on her. Hah! They'd need to try better than that. At first, she was surprised by the other suitors' coordination, but then she remembered that they all had their windsuits' power activated, and were communicating through their headsets.

Then another windsuiter dove at her, a streak of blue passing right before Corey's eyes. What lunacy was this? Were Dree's windsuiters trying to tackle her in midair? They were flying at hundreds of miles per hour: a collision could be deadly. Were Corey and her charge really worth Dree workers risking their lives? Apparently so. To Dree, workers were disposable. It was one of the many reasons Corey was leaving in the first place.

More suits swiped at Corey. She weaved around turbines and even flew between their spinning blades in an attempt to lose them, but it was no use. The flock behind her steadily approached: their flying V formation allowed each to follow in the slipstream of the one ahead, reducing wind resistance. But she could feel herself being lifted by Asda's gravity. She was nearly there. She had one last idea to throw them off her tail. She flew directly into the puffy white cloud.

Immediately the noise of her environment dampened. She became aware of her rushed breathing, and tried to calm herself. Aside from the mist forming on her visor, her entire field of vision was shades of white: when she turned her head, she could hardly see her feet in the mist. Behind her, she had seen the flock of windsuiters peel away, not entering the cloud. Perhaps they were too worried about staying in formation, thinking the confusion of the cloud would cause them to collide with each other. Corey found that she no longer had to tilt herself to generate lift to counteract the gravity of Marda. She was floating. For the moment, everything was peaceful.

Her breathing steadied and her stomach lurched. She felt herself now falling up: Asda's gravity had taken control. Yes! Now she just had to let herself fall onto the transiting moon, and then she'd be free.

Then she was caught by something hanging in the air. Ack! She flailed around, trying to extract herself from the net, but she only ended up getting more tangled. The net cushioned her for a few seconds, until she slammed into it, having reached the end of its tension. Then she felt herself being pulled up and out of the cloud. Her brief excursion into Asda's gravity well had not gone well. She scrambled to unseal her pocket.

Corey was being pulled faster now, as she returned to Marda's gravity. She tried to stand but the net was too unsturdy, opened her arms to generate lift but the net was moving too fast. She felt her other pockets for a knife but found nothing: it was essential to travel light in a windsuit. The fibers of the netting were too thick to cut anyway. She was trapped.

Then the cloud disappeared from around her. She was surrounded by windsuiters. Some dressed in grey held the sides of the net, circling around Corey to prevent escape. That flock of windsuiters wasn't afraid of losing formation in the cloud, they'd known about the net! And the grey specks Corey had seen around the cloud wasn't falling Asdan terrain, it was grey windsuiters holding the net, just waiting for her to fall into their trap! Corey cursed herself. She'd been so stupid! Dree was the most powerful corporation in the star system, of course, they'd be able to stop one stupid windsuiter. They had infinite resources, and Corey didn't have infinite wit.

The circling windsuiters descended onto the barge and deposited Corey unceremoniously onto the wet deck with a thud. A pair of boots stepped in front of her vision, and behind them, blue and grey windsuiters alighted on the ship. Further on, the cloud between Asda and Marda split in two, and the bulging ocean settled down again. Asda's perigee had come to an end.

"How embarrassing." The voice from the loudspeakers sounded less distorted, coming from right in front of her. "Caught by a simple net."

"I hate you," Corey said. It was quieter than she'd intended.

"Ah, but the people love us," the owner of the boots said. "We provide for Marda, for the entire star system. Everyone knows Dree Inc. as a saintly company."

"They'll hate you, too," Corey said. "Once they know what

Dree really does."

The boots paused in thought. "Cut her out of the net. Put her in restraints and search her." The suiters did as they were told. Arms grabbed at her, held her, searched her, but there was no longer anything to find. Corey was too exhausted to put up a fight, but it didn't matter anyway. She was caught, but she'd won.

Trapped in the cloud, she'd opened her pocket and flung the data drive through a hole in the net. It faded into the gloom instantly, but she knew that it had fallen to the surface of Asda. Someone would find it, she knew, and they'd see all the information Corey had stolen. Dree's corruption, the way they treated employees, the many, many violations of Mardan and star system law, the absolute evil they'd purveyed while putting on a perfectly innocent, friendly facade: the news would spread around the star system. They would be caught, just like they had Corey caught. This was the end for Corey, but only the beginning of the end for Dree Incorporated.

Dree would call what she was doing theft, but all she was doing was making information more free. And soon Marda would be free, too.

Something Funny

Yiyang Zhang

It's an ordinary afternoon, and you're at an ordinary public gym. There's a guy there, twenty-ish, and he's wearing a t-shirt two sizes too large. It's bright orange and lined with white vinyl wording, too faded to read but obviously designed as a free promotional fashion. The man is smaller. He's the height of an average American woman and weighs that of an average American child. He's got the worst posture you've ever seen on a human person.

Next to him at the free weight section, there's another man. Huge, this one. He has shoulders like the World Trade Center, and there are veins on his forearms you thought existed only in comic books. He's breathing like a Minotaur—repping out the weights of only slightly lighter livestock. The smaller man—noticing this—picks up his own neon dumbbell, turns to the beast, and says, "Please, don't be intimidated by me. We were all beginners once."

Here's another situation. You're at a bar with a few friends—chatting, laughing. It's a good time. One of your friends is making a lot of jokes, most of them about his being single. He's always single. He knows it. He knows it's him and his issues. He even says that "he would explain why, but it'd take the rest of the night." Everyone laughs.

The issue is that he sort of really means it. He sort of really always means it. But it's hard. The really sticky stuff—the feeling stuff—it's hard to talk about. It's messy and gooey, kind of gross. He'd rather be funny.

The issue with that is that it makes it hard to be alone. You can't really be that funny with just yourself. Jokes about your mom who prefers your sister don't really land the same. When he tries, he just feels kind of sad. There's nowhere for all the messy, sticky stuff to go. And those are the moments he really, really wants to be around people. Any people. Even the friends he doesn't really feel all that close to anymore—when they invite him for something, he's eager. This time, they invited him for drinks and movies. He said yes. Very loudly. He sounded a little panicked.

The movie's nice—loud, colorful, dazing. He loves these kinds of movies. They make you forget your name and feel good about everything. Anything that's not on the screen—it's okay. Life is bigger and further and easier in the theater. Just watch. He knows how to watch. The actors are also really attractive— symmetrical and scary. Seeing their pretty faces contort to express something human is exciting, emotional in ways that cost nothing. It makes his life feel less like everything. He feels less like himself watching the pretty actors—feels bigger and bolder. He even considers grazing the hand of the girl next to him—the pretty one his friends keep trying to set him up with. Everything is possible in the theater.

Afterward, he finds himself sitting between these friends and their loud post-movie discussion. He feels like himself again. It's not a good thing. You can imagine it like crashing after a long fall—feeling for once so, so weightless and sweet about everything and then in another second, splatting into something earthly and indifferent. All the sticky, difficult stuff is still there—all inside him. It's all happening inside him. His friends are still laughing. He remembers why they're not that close anymore. His beer looks like piss. It's reflective. The bottle makes the world look tawny. He's not saying anything. The sounds from his friends—even those from the cute girl he sort of likes—seem muffled and alien. The girl laughs a lot. Her eyes are kind of uneven.

How long has that man been working out?

They're making jokes about how single he is. He knows they're trying to help. He hates himself for being quiet. He offers

158

something funny–something easy. They all laugh, but he regrets saying it. It wasn't honest–what he said. He said it because they would laugh, and then he wouldn't have to really talk to them. He wouldn't have to deal with them. They would just laugh and leave him to himself. Does he want to be alone?

Definitely not. He knows that. It's just hard to say the things that he really means. It's like—in a very serious way—like being naked. People see you—very much they see you, all skin and fat–but it takes a lot of guts. It takes a lot of steel and desperation to lay yourself flat like that—let people stare at you. But if he poses, if he jokes, if he paints himself up and makes it not so real, he's still showing himself—naked—all of it. He's just not being vulnerable. It's only meaning it—really truly lying on your back and just saying the thing—that's ever made anyone vulnerable.

That's why irony is so tricky. It gives the textural feeling of being naked—being bare and honest and personal–just without all of the mush, without all the eye contact. Jokes are how you can talk about the sticky stuff–every hard emotional wiring and not feel gross, not be embarrassed. Of course, the performance of it does feel a little gross.

It feels exploitative, but it works really well. Everyone is laughing. So he doesn't stop. Loneliness makes him selfish. And he really doesn't ever want to be alone. He'd crumple so fast. And nobody wants that. It's unnatural. There are always higher ambitions. He has higher ambitions. How could he stop?

Later that night, stuff comes up. He's panicked. He's breathing really heavily—like his body is working to catch up to his mind. It's quiet. The air is cold and dry. What it adds up to–this quietness and heavy breathing—is a very loud and very scary panging, right against his sternum. It's punchy and uneven and again to reiterate really, really scary because the panging is coming from inside himself, and that means there's nothing to remove, nothing to scrub away at.

He regrets saying that thing at the bar. Who was he to do that? Who was he to humor and relate to those he doesn't understand? What must all that performance say about him?

He thinks of his mother and what she would say, not his actual mother who was very cruel and unsympathetic to his young inconvenient anxieties, but for the mother he as a small, scared child imagined her to be if only his personality were less inconvenient, more like his sister. Lying in the dark, he imagines a woman—prettier and chubbier than his real mother—rocking him and hushing him in that loving whispery way older women do so well. Sometimes he thinks everything sad is about mothers.

It's really quiet tonight. He stays still. He doesn't want to disrupt anything. His friends probably didn't mean their laughing either. They have their own stuff. Why doesn't he ever think of that? He hates himself for not thinking of that. He never thinks of the things that he so wants to believe when he so needs to believe them.

He thinks of the bar table. He thinks of its stool chairs–slightly too long for him, and how it was there they all sat and made nothing but jokes and half-laughs. For hours. Sitting on long stools, masses of thought and fallen nature—too entangled in their own ego and tricky feelings to risk anything honest.

He turns his head against the pillow. It's gotten hot. The cotton smells chemical and botanic. It's rough against his cheek.

His mother would say he's pathetic. He is a little ashamed. This is a lot of goo, and he suspects all it's really doing is hurting his feelings.

Maybe that's the whole thing–the whole issue of his being a feeling animal. It's made him vulnerable to goo, hungry for sap. Because he has higher ambitions—way too many higher ambitions. He really wants them though. He really wants them all. He wants to laugh and mean it. He wants to clap when something good happens. He wants to hold a girl's hand and make steamy, long eye contact because it's nice and she's pretty, and he's red-blooded, and he can. He wants all the lovely things that come with being a person. He wants to be honest. But that stuff takes guts. Getting naked means letting yourself be cold and believing someone's going to come cover you. It's a lot. And you can get really cold. How can he ever expect to know people the way he knows himself without loving them the same too? The panging is really fast now.

He thinks of the girl—the one his friends like for him. He thinks of her hands, how he wished he had touched them, and how he wished that would change anything. She is pretty. If only he had touched her hand and had said something sweet— something she'd like. He would have had her. They could have gone home together. She could have been sitting with him right now. She could have been holding his hand right now and looking at him kindly.

She would have been making jokes. He would have been laughing—not really understanding her, not really caring too. She wouldn't notice. They would have watched another movie together. The movie would be good. All the characters would be pretty; their lives would be neat. And they'd both be lying and scared, but they'd be together. They'd be laughing.

An Unexpected Uber

Sam Cooper

It was a typical Friday evening, and I was ordering an Uber to my friend's apartment for a party. I would have walked if it hadn't been for my aching knee wrapped tightly in a knee brace. Ever since I regrettably squatted well over my previous record, I had found myself feeling constant, nagging pain that effectively made casual walking a nuisance. Since being diagnosed with Bursitis in my right knee, I had been ordering Ubers to keep both my knee and my mental health intact.

As I opened the Uber app and requested a ride, I only thought of future conversations I would have with my close friends, how much I would drink, and what time I'd like to go home. With no thought of my present and only considering my plans for the night, I had no clue that this next Uber ride would become a formative experience in my second semester at the University of Virginia.

The car arrived and I hopped in the backseat. I was greeted by a friendly smile from the driver as he gave a warm hello. He introduced himself as John and asked how my day had been.

With my knee, problems with friends back home, issues with finding a date to my upcoming formal, and extreme stress from my extracurriculars and school work, I sighed deeply and gave an honest answer, "It hasn't been going well, man. But, everything could be worse, and I'm grateful for all I have." I wasn't lying. This has been my philosophy for the past three years of my life since the pandemic hit and my family contracted COVID-19 and went into lockdown. Nonetheless, I usually save my philosophical theories for my close friends; however, something about John enabled me to pass along one of my virtues.

From that point, I could feel the energy change within the car. I felt comfortable regaling him with stories of my dad—the source of many of my life values. He listened when I explained how my dad was different from other "wrestling dads" in that he stands at 5 foot 7 inches and weighs no more than 150 pounds with a soft spot for the grateful dead, meditating, and carving pineapple. John and I laughed as he recounted memories of intense sporting parents he met in high school when he played basketball in Michigan.

The world passed around me faster than ever in this car, and I realized five minutes had passed in what felt like 30 seconds. I was almost upset at myself for hogging the conversation, as I had a gut feeling that John had unique and riveting stories. Therefore, I searched my mind for a quick, yet deep question. Waiting for a small break in the conversation as we hit a red light, I crafted the perfect conversation starter to add a layer of personal connection to our newly founded relationship. "What lessons in your life have you carried with you today?" Immediately after posing the question, I scolded myself for not wording my sentence better to reflect what I meant to ask him. Could I have been more specific? Will he understand what I meant? Is he going to tell me a fascinating tale from his past? This time, only a minute later from my realization, I was waiting in anticipation for seconds that seemed like hours.

John and I simultaneously glanced at his Google Maps app that said we had only six minutes left in the car. Nonetheless, John understood and obliged my question and began telling me about growing up in Michigan and traveling all over the country. John graduated from high school and attended a four-year university like me; however, the similarities ended there. Shortly after graduating from the University of Connecticut, he moved to Illinois to live with his girlfriend at the time who was finishing up her degree at the University of Illinois Chicago. After her graduation, they moved to be closer to some of John's family in Wisconsin, and he proposed to her. John and his fiance married a year later and had a boy; however, money was tight for them. They both pursued degrees in education, and money became an area of contention in their marriage. As soon as John explained this, he paused. "We fought some nights over how we should spend, but I didn't think our relationship was permanently damaged…that was until I came back from work with a letter that said 'Dear John'." That sentence was followed by another pause in the now solemn car ride, as it felt that both of us were on the verge of tears.

In an attempt to break the silence, I asked him in a half-sarcastic, half-serious tone, "Can I hug you?" We both laughed, as John explained that everything in life can change in an instant, and nothing needs to remain the same. He followed that beautiful, deep philosophical thought with another anecdote. "After having my heart broken in two, I decided to travel more. A month had passed since her note, and I was nearly halfway through the Appalachian Trail." John then explained that he learned more while hiking than he did at UConn and proceeded to retell an encounter with his trail buddy, No Rush.

As he began to contextualize No Rush, I realized that I was four minutes away from my destination. I had taken this exact path to my friend Mike's apartment before, but I knew of a shortcut that saved two minutes. While listening to John's tale, I decided I wanted to learn more about No Rush and opted to pay the extra charge of two minutes in his car.

Deciding to fully enjoy my last four minutes with John, I opened my ears and soaked in the moment. He spoke emphatically about No Rush being this mellow, good-natured pothead who's hiked the Appalachian Trail dozens of times since the late 90s. No Rush and John developed a close relationship on the trail, and John ironically realized that he was in no rush to make any strict life plans the more time he spent with his new friend. Traveling with No Rush also reinforced his belief that life can change drastically in an instant, as No Rush contracted an unexpected illness that made him lose all ability to move his right arm. Through this substantial change, No Rush learned how to let go and move on—a lesson John holds dearly to his heart today.

Almost without a moment's notice, the car stopped and John let out a subtle sigh signifying his enjoyment in our short, yet impactful conversation. He and I exchanged a few goodbye words, while I collected my thoughts and walked out the door. His last words to me before driving off were, "Thank you for giving me my best Uber experience yet."

As I watched the car drive away, I reflected on the trip. How can an Uber ride carry so much emotion within a 12-minute time frame? I walked to the door and felt a sense of immense gratitude for the unexpected Uber ride that had brought me closer to a stranger and reminded me of the power of human connection through vulnerability.

Give Me Water

Meghan Parry

The first thing you need to know is that it wasn't my fault. It's true, there's a long list of unsavory deeds with my name on it that I won't even try to explain away, but what went down at the docks, that wasn't me. I can tell you who did do it though. Later. Second thing to know: this is a story about a simple guy called "Poe" because I can make my words as sweet or sour, soft or sharp, as I want 'em and because, other than that, there's not much else to say about me. Yeah, someone thought they were real smart for knowing about an obscure guy like Edgar Allen Poe. I don't really know why it happened but, when they referenced my resemblance to him, the name stuck like a rusted-over nut, parched for oil, that won't come loose from the bolt no matter how many times you crank the wrench.

Well, I'm not a poet. I'm just a conman with a silver tongue who is as lost in this dull, lifeless world as the rest of us. Remember that long list of my old crimes? Talked my way out of at least fifty of the little ones. Things like murder are slightly harder to squirm your way out of with words, yeah, but come up with a convincing story as an alibi and it does the trick more times than not. If not, there are a hundred other ways to grease the system and keep yourself out of the cooler and, as you might've guessed, I'm more than familiar with all of them—plus all the extra sins you need to commit to make them happen. I can admit to all that yeah, but while I might be far from innocent, what happened at the docks, that wasn't my fault.

Third thing, the night they took the traitor down to the docks

166

and strangled him I, miraculously, have a legit alibi this time. I was stealing from the fat pigeons in the new sky casino, the oasis for the rich that's surrounded by everyone else's desolate, dirt-dry reality. A truly superlative feat of human engineering. And of course the perfect market for my kind. It's all too easy to work anything out of the insatiable fools in that temperature-controlled, just bright and just dark enough room where all the gambling leaves the taste of disappointment and adrenaline on the tip of your tongue like overly expensive alcohol that's worse than the cheap stuff. I made over 50,000 credits that night in earrings and bracelets and antique watches I pilfered with no one the wiser. Even to me, that's not pocket change. Enough to buy a couple dozen gallons of pristine spring water. I can still remember the one and only time I tasted clear, fresh water like that. It was like I'd been given a sip of pure life from the kind of mystical fountain the real ancient poets and storytellers used to write about.

That's my favorite part about reading pre-depression authors—imagining the world they talk about where water would run in rivers over the land and fall in tiny drops from the sky, so clean you could drink it as it fell on your tongue. A world where ships would actually sail on oceans of the stuff instead of this endless, black, empty space.

Me and Max, we used to fantasize about that blessed world a lot whenever he rummaged around in my stuff and pulled out some relic that sparked his curiosity, and he came running to me with a million questions. Our dreams would be of blue-green seas sparkling under the midday sun. First time I met him, he was shouting about water like it was God's salvation.

"Please! Give me water, please!" His hands were gripping the front of my shirt, the highest he could reach while slumped on his knees in the city's gristle. He was so dried out by the summer heat he could barely hold himself up and the poor kid, grasping me, trying to force me to stay and hear his pleas, was in fact leaning on me for balance. When he swayed, I felt his weight tugging at me, pulling me forward.

His face was twisted and if he'd had a drop to spare, he

would've been weeping.

That was back when I used to run errands for the belt mafia. I was slick and smooth, I moved with the stealth of a lean cat. I was confident. Best of all, I was good at storytelling, when I needed a story. If I ever ran into a patrol, I could spit out an improvised excuse faster than you can spit out an old cigarette, and it would convince any overly suspicious beat cop tryin' to prove themselves worthy of more than the low-grade life they've got, no problem. But having that skill was practically useless because I never got caught by those amateurs that call themselves police. I could move product, water, you name it, stuffed into the back of my rust-red Stingray 2000, anywhere on Mars, and even all the way to one of Jupiter's moons for the right

price. I was their favorite guy, best of the best. Being a criminal is in your blood, thoroughly scorched into your bones with an aching, slow-burning fire, a brand you learn to forget when you grow up like me.

I don't know how he knew. No cop ever knew, but somehow Max could tell I had a quality gallon stashed in my bag. It was even in a soundproof container so you couldn't hear the delicious, almost musical sloshing.

Put any money-bloated elite in front of me and I'll put two bullets right where his rotted heart would be if he even had one and I'd do it without blinking. But put a hard, hungry, disgusting, scrappy, forgotten piece of dirt survivor of this shit world in front me and I go and steal a pint from the goddamn mafia for the kid. My heart still lies down there in the grime and grit no matter how high into the sky I've climbed.

Number one rule on the streets: when someone crosses you, you give 'em twice what they gave you. But I'm a live-in-the-moment kind of guy. And watching Max guzzle that whole pint right in front of me, like a drowned man gulping in a breath of air, like an animal wolfing down its meal before the predator lurking in the shadows crept out and crushed its throat, I could– just for one damned second– ignore the consequences that would come from breaking that rule. From then on, Max was on my heels wherever I walked and in my passenger seat whenever I flew like he was some kind of sad-eyed, red-haired puppy.

He was with me for the rest of the short time I stayed with the belt mafia. He was messing around in my stingray one time, trying to straighten up the perpetual wreck I keep it in when he found the frayed book of poetry I forgot about in one of the million little compartments next to the pilot's seat. He must've liked it too because the next time I made a particularly eloquent joke to one of the mafia's bruisers, Max chimed in, "That was better than Mr. Poe!", and I said, "Mr. Poe? The hell is that?", and he whipped out the book then and there, threw it open to the page he wanted and pointed at the title: "The Raven". Just below that, in faded black print, was the name "Edgar Allen Poe". After that, I honestly didn't know what to say. Neither did anyone else. Until they all burst out laughing. Max could be such an absurd kid sometimes that there was nothing you could do but laugh an incredulous, irrepressible laugh. Incredulous at the innocence that still exists in the world, perhaps as the rarest commodity of them all. So precious and beautiful I sometimes thought to myself I'd die to protect it.

We were hanging out with a bunch of low-level mafiosos at the time. We were in the common room of one of the belt mafia's massive cruisers, dozing on the couches, drinking, smoking, playing with frail cards, fiddling with tools, and doing maintenance on her that she didn't really need. While the rest of us were listless and unwilling to move more than we had to, Max was asking me question after question under his breath about the cruiser. It was his first time in a ship other than my stingray and there was a genuine glint of excitement in his eyes as he marveled at the sheer size and weight of her. And, yeah, he had a point. The mafia's gear is top of the line and she was a marvel even to my veteran's eyes. Only problem with these big ships are the rats. But I didn't tell Max about the rats. I knew he would ask and he didn't need to know so I didn't tell him, that's all.

Anyway, a bunch of people heard and now everyone can only remember me as Poe. I bet you if you asked them about Bruce, they'd wrinkle their ugly noses at you and say, "Who the hell is that?"

That was a long time ago now, before I split with them, Max trailing along behind me. Guess they never forgot me, even with all that wishful thinking I did.

"I give water, I take it. And now I'll drain every drop of it in your worthless body before I throw you to the rats and let them eat you down to your bones."

There were eight guys there, all bruisers, all thick with muscle, all itching for violence, all staring down the person who betrayed them and confessed to it all.

"You were stupid to think you could steal from me."

The biggest of them all was once known by everyone as a professional boxer whose name earned the fear it commands through bloody win after bloody win. It was decades ago but he'd only cultivated that learned, hammered-in hardness, used it to make himself a leader. A leader who knew how brutal leaders have to be. He wasn't just punishing the kid with his cursing and his taunting. He was putting on a show in front of the others. That's what you do when you make an example of someone.

Max took all of the abuse, only hanging his head, red hair hiding his eyes, inscrutable, and saying nothing.

"Now what were you, thinkin' boy? Thought I wouldn't notice it was missin'? Thought I wouldn't care? What kind of boss would I be if I let lying thieves take what's mine?!"

The last line was a sudden roar. Spittle flew from his mouth as he raged. He sneered like a wolf bearing its teeth in front of its victim. One of the other men snatched a fistful of the boy's hair and held him up for the boss, who clamped a meaty hand around Max's thin neck and pulled him even closer to see the fear in his wretched eyes. Max was so small, his toes just barely scraped the ground as he dangled from their grip. They stared at each other, but even though his pale eyes were bloodshot and he was gasping for breath, the fight in Max's eyes still blazed like fire. So that unforgiving hand squeezed harder.

Max stayed quiet and stubborn until the end. Didn't change

the story he'd given them, that he was so thirsty, that he couldn't help himself. That he'd just wanted a taste of the water.

And while they were down there in the shadows between two ships watching Max's skinny little body be consumed piece by piece, you were having fun pilfering jewelry off men and women in bright clothes, planning to use the money to buy some new parts for your stingray. Thought maybe you and Max would go on a little trip, go see Saturn's rings in person. You wanted to see if they were really as divine as they looked the first time Max saw them in some documentary. At first, you didn't want to watch it but Max was enjoying himself so you watched anyway from the kitchen, far enough away to pretend you weren't watching. Far enough away that Max couldn't see you smile at the absurdity of his childish enthusiasm.

You couldn't have known they'd found out, that someone had seen and cracked. You couldn't have know Max would take the blame, shield a stupid, selfish criminal like you. So, it was the snitch's fault. It was the boss's fault. You might even be shitty enough to whisper to yourself that it was Max's fault. But it was never your fault. It wasn't.

The Speculator

Samson McCune

Grant watched the forest through the smoke of his morning fire. Deep within the Unexplored Lands, he was lost. It had been so long since the last time that he had known where he was that he hardly even considered it in such ways anymore. The word 'lost' no longer had any meaning. Now, he just lived. Now, disconnected from the binding of society, he was free.

He took the squirrel from where it was being cooked and ate. Above, the gray skies shifted through the needles of pine that patterned the heavens. The world was beautiful. Alone and secluded from the rest of society, Grant almost wished that he had never even been introduced to civilization. It was too complicated, too stressful.

There had hardly been a day in his life since he had broken away from the curses of other people that he hadn't woken up with a smile on his face and an unyielding sense of gratitude.

When he had had his fill—around half of the squirrel—he gave the rest to Bert. Bert was a good dog. He deserved more than the squirrel, but any more than what he was eating would fatten him up, and that would only make his life harder.

Momentary joy didn't outweigh long-term happiness.

The pair sat and watched the fire as it fizzled out. When it was done, Grant cleaned up camp and packed his things.

"Should we try to get to the top today?" Grant asked Bert when he was done.

Bert tilted his head and panted as if to say "If that's where our feet take us."

172

Grant laughed. Bert was the best kind of companion. He never argued, never treated him with disrespect, and was always there when Grant needed someone to talk to.

They wandered through the forest for a bit, stepping over fallen logs and kicking their way through piles of dead pine needles. Grant took a deep breath and couldn't stop a smile from forming on his face. These were the times that he felt most alive.

Bert had been a pup when they had first traveled out into the Unknown Lands, hoping to become famous speculators for the Dinsh. Back then, Grant had been full of rage and fear. Back then, Bert had been a burden.

Grant cringed when he thought about how he had been, especially to Bert. His dream of being a famous speculator had been founded on the idea that that was the only way he could contribute to society, that without his job, he would be useless.

What an unhealthy way to live.

They came to a stop in front of a small, but rapid, stream. "Maybe this is a sign?"

Bert slurped up water, which clearly meant "It definitely could be," in dog.

Grant rubbed Bert behind the ears as he drank and looked up and downstream to see which way was more favorable. To descend would be easier, or that was the way it appeared. However, perhaps more importantly, Grant wasn't in the mood for something easy today. He wanted to challenge himself, and as such decided that today they would try to make their way to the top.

This wasn't the first time that they had tried. Every other attempt had been barred by roadblocks and unforeseen dangers, so they had been abandoned. Reaching the top had never been so desirable that Grant would have risked his or Bert's lives over it. He hoped that this time would be different. Not that it mattered, though. It was just something that he wanted to do, not his purpose.

Bert sniffed the ground expectantly. "Upstream, it is then?" he almost seemed to ask.

"Upstream," Grant agreed.

They followed the creek's path from a few paces away. Even from the distance, Grant could see specks of krut glittering in the water. He smiled as he imagined what Unknown Lands would look like had people known about its existence there. Krut. One of the scarcest and most important resources to the Dinsh. Every politician, every farmer, every merchant, wanted to get their hands on it.

He wasn't any different in this regard. That's why he had become a speculator. Krut would have guaranteed him a life of wealth and prosperity. What a good thing it was that he realized there was more to life than money.

Gradually, the ground became steeper. They were coming closer to Mount Freedom, as he liked to call it. It was strange not seeing it from a distance. Most of his travels had taken him around it, and as such, it was always visible in the distance. Now, standing on it, he felt only as he had a few other times in his life.

It was like a feeling of loneliness mixed with a sense that something was off.

There was no path, so Bert and Grant had to make their own way through the forest. There were few times at lower altitudes that the terrain ever got rough enough to necessitate climbing or balance, but the higher they climbed, the more that changed. Boulders and other rocks were scattered about. Usually, they could just be avoided.

It was rare that something so obstructive as a cliff would appear, yet today it seemed that that was exactly the case. The pair walked along the edge of it with hopes of finding a shallower grade to ascend and only found that the cliff increased in height the further they went.

"Should we try to climb?" Grant asked.

Bert frowned and looked at his paws. "I can't."

Grant pursed his lips and tried to think. Bert couldn't climb, but that didn't mean that their day was ruined. There still had to be a way to reach the top.

"What should we do?"

"Maybe we can go back the other way to see where that goes,"

Bert offered.

As usual, Bert was exactly on point. There was no need to get upset without exhausting all available options, and even then, the world was still beautiful. Grant was confident that he could even find gratitude in failure.

They walked the other way this time, and like the other side, this cliff grew higher the further they went. It appeared that the lowest point had been where they had made first contact.

Was this the end? As much as he didn't want it to be so, Grant was starting to think that it was. The cliff walls glimmered with krut, almost teasing Grant for making the decision not to become a speculator. The profits would have been nearly endless with its help.

He smirked and traced his fingers along a particularly prominent vein as an idea formed in his mind. Krut's usefulness was much different than gold's, which relied on its durability over time and beauty. Krut had both power and utility, and both of these things were unlike anything that the world had ever seen.

For one, it could respond to the will of the user. Grant had only used it once or twice, and each time it had given him something extraordinarily small. There were, of course, rumors about the other things that krut could do, although he had never been able to verify those things.

"Could we have a path to the top?" Grant asked while he was touching the almighty krut.

At first, nothing happened. Grant didn't mind. Sometimes those things took time. Bert panted happily by his side, as patient as ever. The pair were of the idea that one of the problems with people was their impatience. They had worked very hard to distance themselves from this vice.

They watched the forest as they waited, wondering if they might see some wildlife. Bert had been craving squirrel ever since his small portions in the morning and was hoping that he would have the opportunity to catch another.

Grant turned around and saw that there was now a cave in the cliff wall that appeared to ascend to the peak of the mountain.

The krut had worked faster than he had expected. What a pleasant surprise.

"You ready?" he asked.

Bert licked his chops. "Of course."

They walked inside and became enveloped by the darkness before they knew it. Caves were quite good at blocking light from Grant's experience. He and Bert had been in a great deal of them, and every single one of them had been both wet and dark. Oddly, even though this one hadn't been formed by erosion, it was as well.

Stalagtites grew from the ceiling, dripping to create stalagmites. Grant couldn't help but stop and admire the view. Caves were truly amazing things. Their success was a testament to how nothing good came without hard work and tenacity.

They hiked upwards for some time, mostly without the aid of their eyes. Bert was quite good at navigating in the dark as he could use his nose to avoid the walls. However, Grant wasn't so lucky. Instead, he chose to hold on gently to Bert's tail and follow him that way. He knew not to squeeze too hard, though, as the dog didn't like his tail being touched.

Gradually, the cave brightened. They were nearing the top. Grant's curiosity spiked the closer they got. What would be at the exit? Would they be any closer to the top of Mount Freedom, or would an entirely new set of challenges face them? With excitement, the pair finished their ascent to find out.

Harsh light blinded them momentarily. Coming out of caves was always like that. Grant imagined that people's eyes weren't designed to go from so dark to so bright so fast. He was lucky that it was overcast, though. Otherwise, the shift might have been painful and more difficult.

What he saw shocked him. It wasn't supposed to be like this. It had been years since he had been so disappointed. Grant shot Bert a pleading look, hopeful that his eyes were deceiving him, but the way the dog's hackles rose told him that they were looking at the same thing.

There was a Dinsh colony on the top of the mountain.

Grant dove back against the wall. "Please, don't be there when I look back," he whispered. It had to be a bad dream. He had to have imagined it. Carefully, he peaked back out to confirm his fears.

All around, people bustled. Some mined krut, while others chopped trees and constructed more-than-temporary shelters. Grant looked around to see if he could recognize any of the invaders, but it had been so long since the last time that he had seen somebody other than Bert that they all looked the same to him: evil.

He wanted to turn and run and never come back. This discovery meant the end of everything he valued. All of his freedoms, all of his happiness and joy would now be taken away by the empire that had deprived him of those feelings in the first place.

What were he and Bert supposed to do now? Where could they run? Deeper into the Unknown Lands would be dangerous, and back to the Dinsh would mean giving up. Not to mention that Grant was starting to think of the forest as his home. There was no reason that he should have to give it up just because some Dinsh came. His utopia would not be ruined.

One look at Bert told him that they were having the same thoughts. They would have to fight. Running wasn't an option. Neither of them wanted to look over their shoulder for the rest of their lives, hoping that they wouldn't find the demons of Din on their tails.

Quickly and quietly, Grant and Bert made as much distance as they could between them and the colony. They would have to be fast, in both their planning and the execution of it. The Dinsh weren't known for being lackadaisical when constructing colonies, and especially not so when krut was involved.

Grant estimated that the Dinsh had no more than a week before their fortifications became impossibly difficult to destroy. Bert, as supportive as he was, insisted that they only had six days, so they agreed upon attacking on day six instead of seven. Better to work together and have one less day than disagree and fail as a result.

Grant hated everything about living in Din. Clouds of coal filled the air, blocking out the sun and the happiness that it brought with it. Bleak. That was the word he had been thinking of before he had picked up the bundle that he now held in his arms.

The pup wiggled, trying to escape his grip, but he held on. It was too small and weak to go out on its own. Maybe when it was stronger, he would let it choose whether to stay or to go. Nobody should have to feel trapped. Freedom was the greatest boon that someone could be granted.

This wasn't what he wanted, he realized. He didn't want to be Dinsh, and he definitely didn't want to work for them and their destructive concepts. He wanted to live for himself and his happiness, not somebody else's.

He went through the motions of the rest of his day and was about to go to sleep when he heard whining. Confused, he tried to find where it was coming from. Was someone hurt? His apartment saw strange things, but he had never heard such long, drawn-out cries of pain.

That was when he remembered the newcomer: the dog. With a grimace, he raced around the house, searching for the only thing that his sister had entrusted him with before leaving.

And there it sat in the middle of his kitchen. It probably smelled the ghosts of food that had once been. What a young, weak thing to still be unable to control its hunger pangs. Grant had long since learned to ignore them himself.

"You want something to eat?" he asked the dog.

The dog tilted its head. Grant might have been going crazy, but it was almost as if that were its way of saying "Yes, please."

"What do you want?"

The dog sniffed the floor and ran around and then fell down panting, which clearly meant "anything." It had quite a bit of energy.

"Let's go see what the city has to offer," he said, picking up the dog.

For a reason that he couldn't understand, he packed a bag before leaving. In it, he carried only the essentials: his last bits of food, a lighter, a knife, and a speculation compass.

He never knew where his feet might take him next.

It was late, so most of the restaurants were closed. Grant considered trying the grocery store or the farmer's market, both of which stayed open far later than the former, but before he knew it he had passed both by.

Instead, he hailed a cab and presented the driver with his speculator's license. He had hardly understood his decision until he was standing on the border of Din and the Unknown Lands. Again, he had to present the government with his speculator's license.

When he stepped through the mist, a cage that had been surrounding him his entire life broke, and he felt a sense of clarity that he had never felt before. Free from the bleakness and dirtiness of Din, he was now able to live how he wanted.

A thought struck him. "What do you think of the name Bert?" he asked the puppy, who seemed to be quite a bit more excited about this new turn of events than he was.

"I love it."

Mist hung in the air. Grant and Bert moved through it silent as ghosts as they approached the Dinsh camp. They hadn't spoken at all since waking up, almost as if talking about their undertaking would increase their chances of failure.

Grant's backpack was heavy with equipment that he hoped he wouldn't have to use. The further they followed their plans, the less fortunate the situation was. Ideally, the Dinsh would just be gone when they arrived and everything would be okay. For some reason, Grant doubted that that would be the case.

And when he looked, there stood the Dinsh colony. High and mighty it stood, stronger than Grant would have expected after even fifteen days. How were they going to succeed? Their plan was starting to feel hopeless. There was no use trying to stop this from happening. The Dinsh were too powerful.

But then he looked at Bert and the conviction in his eyes. This was what they needed to do. The Dinsh didn't belong, and they had no right to take Grant and Bert from their found Utopia.

"Are you ready?" he asked Bert before they left for their attack.

The dog nodded. Their plan was short but powerful. Colonies operated chiefly on water supply, for both power and sustenance. All they had to do to win was divert the source, and the Din would have nothing to eat, nothing to use to power the mining equipment that would provide them with krut. If that didn't do enough to drive them away, they would break their machinery as best as they could. Infrastructure was the core of a colony.

The pair climbed as high as they could while also tracing the stream that had led them to the Dinsh colony. The cave was the only way up, so they had to be careful not to be caught once they were near the settlement. Strangely enough, though, it looked like the place was empty. Not a sound could be heard from within.

In the heat of the moment, Grant ignored this irrationality and continued up the mountain. This was it. He could finally be free from their greed and hostility. All he had to do was destroy one colony and everything would be fine.

Atop the mountain, there sat a spring. It wasn't nearly as beautiful as Grant would have expected, although the view was something else entirely. He imagined that he could see from one end of the plot to the other up there. The horizon beckoned in the best way, reminding him of the innate curiosity that drove him to leave Din in the first place.

He and Bert carved a scar into the mountain with care and love, fully aware of the impact that they would have on the area. Not only did this particular spring feed the Dinsh, but it fed into a few smaller streams and made a river. Many animals went to it and its tributaries for their own needs. As a result of this, the balance in the forest would shift, but that was okay. The land would recover, and even better now that the Dinsh were gone.

As they were cutting into the ground, Grant realized something. From the top of Mount Freedom, he could see a ring of trees bordering an opening, almost forming a cage around the peak. Within this opening sat the Dinsh colony. And now he knew that he hadn't been wrong before. It was empty.

His mind raced as he tried to figure out what had happened and he suddenly landed on a realization. Back in the cave, touching the krut-lined walls, he had wished his enemies away.

Looking at the spring and then back at the ghost colony, Grant couldn't help but wonder whether or not that had been because of something that they had done. Had the spring plan been successful? Had the Dinsh somehow caught wind of what he was planning to do and fled as a result?

He didn't know. All that he knew was that there he stood, destroying a part of his happiness for something that didn't matter anymore.

What a fool he had become.

Afterword

This collection that you've picked up, read, and hopefully enjoyed, started as nothing more than a conversation between me and my father. My family has always had an entrepreneurial spirit, with both of my parents owning their own businesses and me recently joining this club, and this comes with the idea that our skills and passions can be monetized.

Fast-forward about a year, and I realize that the idea wasn't only interesting, but it was feasible. These are the two items on my mental checklist for new projects: interesting and feasible. Granted, this realization wasn't birthed out of a vacuum. I had the help of some close friends, too.

During my first semester of college, it was quickly known that I had a publishing company. To some, this meant that I was successful. I wished reality agreed with their perceptions. In truth, I was far from it. The benefit of this talk was that this publicity helped me get one step closer to this dream.

Eventually, some friends came up to me with their idea for a short story contest. My initial answer was that it wasn't feasible, citing the problems that we'd have to work our way through from the website to the legal rights to the work. But every time I told my friends why it couldn't work, they explained to me why I was wrong. I suppose that's what good friends are for helping you learn that many of your limits are self-imposed.

After some deliberation, my friend Ryan Levy and I decided that we would become partners for this project. Our skills complemented each other quite well, making this an ideal working situation.

His work ethic and competency blew me away. It's easy to

forget how incredible people can be. The very night we decided on the rules and outline for the contest, he coded the website to the point that it was already prepared for launch, a month ahead of schedule.

At this point, we started working on how we were going to market it to people. Having a contest is amazing, but how were we going to get people to know about it? And even if they knew what we were offering, would they want to participate?

This was a simple problem of incentive maximization, cost minimization, and being obnoxious about how much we talked about it. Everywhere we went, we put up posters to get people to know about it, which explained that if one were to enter, they could win a spot in a published collection of short stories. Of course, there was also a cash prize, and that certainly helped in the marketing.

April 1st, the launch date, came along and we held our breaths as we watched the submission portal. Was anyone going to want to work with us? Was there a market for small short story contests?

Almost immediately, we got a story. It was surreal, to say the least. Somebody did know about us. On top of that, we didn't know them. Our efforts to share our platform were working and for whatever reason people wanted to compete in our contest.

Over the next few days, we got quite a few more stories. By the 7th we had 10, which was above what we were expecting on the high end. (For reference, in our minds, there was some optimal number of submissions. Twenty stories won, so we wanted twenty at the least, and we had to judge them, so no more than around thirty-five to make that process easy but still selective. This is less than our rate here, with $35/30$ being equal to 1.167 stories per day and $10/7$ being equal to 1.429 stories per day.)

Regardless, our fear that we were getting too many was unfounded. Over the next ten days, we received almost nothing. There was complete radio silence. At this point, we started to wonder what we might do if we didn't even receive twenty submissions. Did we just publish all of them and say that the best among them was the winner of the cash prize? But how could we justify the printing costs in that case? Did we cushion it with short stories written by guest writers? How did we make it fair and still get a full book?

The 21st came along and reminded us that we still had over a week before the contest came to an end. We were getting ahead of ourselves. Another story was submitted and our fears were lessened. This turned out to be the beginning of a trend, and over the next few days, we went from having only ten submissions to a grand total of thirty, which was almost exactly what we wanted. Most of these even came in on the last day, which, in hindsight, was to be expected. It made sense that people would work on something after finding out about it and keep refining it until the last minute.

After this, they had to be judged. This list of thirty stories was sent out to our panel of expert judges, who read them during May and then gave me their ratings for the deadline of June 1st when decisions were released.

Now comes the boring part. The stories were edited, they were reformatted, and now they are in your hands in their final form. It's strange to sit and think about how many collective hours went into this contest.

Hopefully, after reading some of the book, you can see the effort that went into it. Not just the minimal refinements that I made, or the beautiful formatting that you can absolutely thank me for, but for the stories that these authors crafted for you to read. Maybe your friend or family member wrote a story and you bought this book just to read it, or maybe you found out about this and wanted to see what might come of a university short story contest. Either way, I hope that you come out of this with some new thought, some new feeling, some new revelation.

After all, what is a story without someone to inspire?